Pick Your Own Dream Date

the saturday night **bash**

By
Linda Joy Singleton

Lowell 🏠 House
Juvenile
Los Angeles

CONTEMPORARY
BOOKS
Chicago

For good friends and talented writers, Judith Daniels
and Lisa J. Smith:
Thanks for your writing support and for welcoming me
into "The Stress Deadline Club"

Publisher: Jack Artenstein
General Manager, Juvenile Division: Elizabeth D. Wood
Editorial Director: Brenda Pope-Ostrow
Director of Publishing Services: Mary D. Aarons
Senior Editor: Amy Downing
Cover Design: Lisa-Theresa Lenthall
Interior Design: Brenda Leach
Cover Photograph: John Terence Turner/
FPG International

Library of Congress Catalog Card Number: 94-6646

ISBN: 1-56565-143-X

10 9 8 7 6 5 4 3 2 1

How to pick your own dream date:

Get ready for a fabulous party this weekend in *The Saturday Night Bash.* You can dance to a live band, play thrilling games, and enjoy romantic adventures as you pick your own special dream date. Will you clown around with Chad? Get back together with Nathan? Double your fun with Alex? Share sweet kisses with Timothy? Or be swept off your feet by mysterious Devin?

Read about your friends and possible boyfriends on the next three pages. Then begin your weekend adventure on page 7. At the bottom of each page, there will be a choice to make or directions that tell you which page to turn to. Be careful...if you make a wrong decision, your date may be a disaster!

When you reach the end of one story, there's no reason to stop there. Start over again on page 7 and see how many great Saturday night dates you can have! With sixteen possible endings, you're sure to have lots of memorable dates.

Good luck!

4

CAST OF CHARACTERS

You are in the Southern California town of Lowell, where shady trees line neat boulevards, and evergreen hedges and flowering bushes separate the houses. It's a friendly, slow-paced community where smiles and neighborly "hellos" are routine.

The students attend Lowell High, and they are beginning to get impatient for summer to arrive. But there's lots of springtime fun to be had—Emilee Chang is holding her first annual Saturday night bash. Everyone will be there . . . including you!

 *The Girls*

Lori Cramer: Your best friend, Lori is loyal, smart, and fun. Very outgoing with a great sense of humor, Lori doesn't take things too seriously—not even romance. She does have a boyfriend—Bill Sweeney—but they're not that serious. She's involved in more school activities than you can count, but she's especially interested in photography. She's a friend forever . . . unless you betray her.

Tara Lee Tracy: Gorgeous! With long black hair and sparkling green eyes, Tara Lee is one of those people who always looks perfect. Her family moved to California from South Carolina recently, but she's never had a problem making friends—boyfriends, in particular. (However, she may do some scheming at times, so watch out!) She's wild about Nathan Fields, your old boyfriend, and she's afraid he might want you back.

Emilee Chang: Emilee is a modern-day teen with blue-black hair and shining dark eyes. She's confident and lights up a room with her presence, but not too many people know much about the real Emilee. Some of her classmates may call her a snob, but she's really a nice person who cares deeply about her friends. Her parents are from China, but Emilee is a born-and-bred California girl.

Jennifer Wells: Petite and athletic, Jennifer has pretty blue eyes and pale blond hair. Jennifer is a close friend of Emilee's and is so nice that everyone can't help but like her. She's shy around boys and keeps her heart a secret. She feels most comfortable out on the volleyball court, where she can take on any competitor—male or female.

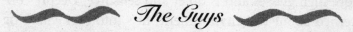 *The Guys*

Nathan Fields: Your former boyfriend, Nathan is blond, tall, and brown-eyed. He's into sports and collects baseball cards. Sometimes he acts really macho, but he's actually very sensitive. You went out with Nathan for three months, and you're afraid you're still hung up on him.

Timothy Cramer: Timothy, Lori's older brother, has wavy auburn hair and hazel eyes, and he's on the shy side. He's smart and super-nice (but can he dance?), and he is editor of the school newspaper. You've known him forever, and you've never noticed him . . . until now.

Chad Estaban: Dark-haired and handsome, Chad is outgoing, athletic, and full of fun. He's always the life of a party, making jokes and clowning around. But he has a secret side to his personality that few people ever see.

Bill Sweeney: Lori's sandy-haired, blue-eyed boyfriend, Bill is very tall and lanky. Although his looks are average, he can sweep a girl off her feet with his dazzling smile and sweet words. He's one of the "in crowd," and he's very friendly with everyone. He also loves to flirt, and if you're not careful, you may get snared in his charming web.

Devin Vargas: He's the mysterious cousin of Emilee's boyfriend, Tyler. Devin is cute and outdoorsy, with dark hair and deep brown eyes. He wears round tortoiseshell glasses and is quiet and sensitive. Deeply concerned about the environment, he's into rock climbing and almost any activity that takes him outside. This is one intense guy!

Alex Reed-Cohen: A phone mix-up may bring Alex into your life. He's medium height, with light brown hair and an easygoing personality. He works part-time for his parents and is close to his brother, Alan.

It's springtime in Lowell, and you're ready for some excitement. There's a warmth in the air, even at night, and the smell of fresh flowers blooming everywhere puts you in a romantic mood—just the type of mood for a party. And, to top it off, you've just been invited to Emilee Chang's Saturday night bash!

Emilee is popular, gorgeous, and super-rich. She lives in a fantastic mansion complete with a video game room, tennis courts, and an indoor, star-shaped swimming pool. You can't believe you're actually going to her house!

You're bursting to share the good news with someone, so you telephone your best friend, Lori Cramer.

"You'll never guess what I got in the mail!" you say, gripping the receiver excitedly.

"Yes I will," Lori replies. "I got one, too."

"An invitation to Emilee's party!" you and Lori shriek together.

"Isn't it great?" you say. "Emilee's parties are famous. I bet she'll have a live band."

"More important," Lori says, her tone suddenly serious, "who are you going to go with?"

 *Turn to **page 29.***

♥ You sigh and struggle with your conflicting emotions. Part of you is hurt that Timothy seems to like another girl. But at the same time, you want Timothy to be happy, and you've never seen him look at a girl the way he's gazing at Jennifer. He must have a major thing for her, and all that stands in his way is you.

*If you suggest that Timothy dance with Jennifer, turn to **page 96.***

*If you ignore Jennifer and dance with Timothy, turn to the **next page.***

Your whole night will be ruined if your date dumps you for someone else. Even though you're not thrilled with dancing with someone who probably has three feet, you tug on Timothy's arm and smile sweetly. "Want to dance?"

He looks away from Jennifer. "I guess so."

The music has slowed to a perfect beat for a slow dance. You lean against Timothy's shoulder and sway gently to the love song.

"Hey, you're a pretty smooth dancer, Timothy," you say, pleasantly surprised that your date has turned out to be such a good dancer.

"You haven't seen anything yet," Timothy says.

The song ends and another begins. This time the tempo is fast and rocking. And as Timothy speeds up his moves, you're amazed at his dancing skill. Wow! You have to work hard to keep up with him.

Timothy twirls you away, then grabs your hand and spins you beneath his arm. Your world tilts and whirls, and you try not to get dizzy. Timothy springs to the ground, then jumps up again, spinning you in another direction.

Other dancers have stopped to watch.

 *Turn to the **next page.***

"Way to go, Tim!" Bill shouts, clapping along with Lori.

Timothy grins. "We're a hit! Let's give our audience a show. Ready for a real workout?"

"Real workout? Isn't that what we've been doing?" you gulp, embarrassed to be out of breath and light-headed. Where did Timothy learn to dance so well?

"Naw. We were just warming up," Timothy says. "Come on! Everyone's watching us."

"I–I want to sit down," you answer.

"*After* we dance," he says cheerfully. Then he grabs you by the waist and hoists you up on his shoulder.

Timothy spins around, and everything blurs before your eyes. You can feel the cherry cola swishing in your stomach, and you try to tell Timothy to put you down. But you're too queasy to talk, and you feel more and more sick every second Timothy whirls.

The room is shaking with clapping and ear-shattering music. You cling to Timothy's shoulder, wishing you had let him dance with Jennifer.

"Oooh," you moan, knowing your face is turning a gross shade of green. If only the room would stop spinning!

When Timothy puts you down, it's too late.

 *Turn to the **next page**.*

You clutch your stomach and double over. Everything is whirling around and around—the colored lights, the floor, and your stomach.

You don't think you can take any more.

You lose it right there. You barf in the middle of Emilee Chang's dance floor. Cherry cola spews like an erupting volcano, and you splatter your new shoes, Emilee's shiny floor, and a few innocent bystanders.

For you, the party's over.

The End

12

♥ You jerk away and slap Bill's face.

"Ouch!" he yelps, rubbing his cheek. "Why did you do that?"

"Because it felt good, and you deserved it," you retort.

"That hurt," he says indignantly.

"Low-life worms like you deserve much worse."

"You're one cold babe. I open my heart to you and you hit me," he says in an innocent little-boy voice.

"You better just hope Lori never finds out what a major creep you are!" you yell.

He raises his brows. "She won't find out unless you tell her."

"Oh, don't worry. I care about her too much to break her heart. Unlike you."

He relaxes and smiles slowly. "So now we share a secret. Let's seal the deal with a kiss."

 *Turn to **page 28**.*

♥ You turn around and hurry away from Chad. As much as you want to ask him to Emilee's party, you just don't have the nerve.

So you continue shopping. You had planned to go to Bodacious Boutique, but you'd have to pass Chad to get there. You check out a trendy new shop instead.

In the window, there's a red-haired mannequin with silver chains draped across her shoulders and squares of thin metal fashioned into a minidress. Very weird. Though you're positive you won't find anything here, you decide to go inside.

"May I help you?" a saleswoman offers. You guess she's in her early twenties. She has a cute smile, and her stylish short hair is almost as red as the mannequin's.

"No, thanks," you say. "I'm just looking."

"Looking for something special?"

"Very special. An outfit for a party."

She smiles widely. "Why not party in one of our unique creations?"

You shake your head. "These styles aren't really me."

"We have something for every individual," she persists. Then before you can protest, she takes you by the hand and leads you to the back of the store. "Come this way."

*Turn to the **next page**.*

The saleswoman pulls a black-and-white dotted outfit off a rack. The material is so shiny you can almost see your reflection. "How about this?" she asks.

"I don't think so. The dots make me dizzy," you say. You tap your foot impatiently. You're sure this is a waste of time. You want to look dazzling at the party, but you suspect everything in this store is too wild for you.

"Aha!" the woman exclaims. "Perfect! This is so *you*. You must try it on."

She holds up a rose-pink miniskirt with an ivory-colored sweater, and you gape in amazement. It is perfect for you. Stylish, sophisticated, and feminine, all at the same time.

You go into the dressing room and try it on. It fits like it was made just for you, and you're thrilled by how great you look.

You glance at the price tag and breathe a sigh of relief. "I'll take it!" you tell the saleswoman.

Five minutes later, the outfit is yours. You thank the saleswoman and walk out of the store.

You're imagining how great you'll look at Emilee's party, when all of a sudden—CRASH! You scream as you fall backward and your bag flies up into the air.

 *Turn to the **next page**.*

From your awkward position on the floor, you look up into a pair of mesmerizing dark eyes.

"I'm sorry," the boy says. "Wow, I completely ran into you. I guess I wasn't watching where I was going. I was cleaning my glasses."

"I wasn't watching, either," you somehow manage to say.

He puts on his round tortoiseshell glasses and holds out his hand, pulling you gently to your feet. The touch of his fingers makes you tingle.

"Here's your bag," he says in a deep voice.

"Thanks." You try to think of something clever and interesting to add, but your mind is blank.

"Are you okay?" he asks.

You nod and grip your bag firmly.

He rakes his fingers through his dark hair. "It isn't every day I literally bowl over a pretty girl. Uh, by the way, my name's Devin."

You like his name. You like his outdoorsy look—a long-sleeved T-shirt, jeans, and big hiking boots. You like everything about him, and you wonder how long you can make this moment linger.

He shuffles his feet and puts his hands into his jeans pockets. "Guess I'd better go. Gotta buy some shoes."

"Well . . . it's been nice bumping into you," you manage to choke out.

He flashes a wide smile. "Same here. Bye."

Then he turns and walks away.

 *Turn to the **next page**.*

16

You stand there for a few moments, watching Devin turn a corner and vanish.

A terrific guy knocks you over and you let him get away! You want to kick yourself for being so shy.

You didn't find out his last name, his phone number, or where he goes to school. You'll probably never see him again, and he doesn't even know your name.

Making a quick decision, you hurry after Devin. Maybe it's not too late. You know he went to a shoe store—how many shoe stores could there be at the mall?

Seven shoe stores.

Thirty minutes later, you're sick of shoes and discouraged. No sign of Devin anywhere. You face the fact that you'll never see him again.

As you leave the mall, you peek into your shopping bag and admire your new clothes. At least today wasn't a total failure. You may have lost Devin, but you found a spectacular party outfit.

X O X O X

By Friday night, you're desperate. You still don't have a date.

Maybe you should call Timothy like Lori suggested. You stare at your bedroom phone. To call or not to call? That's the major question.

Suddenly the telephone rings.

 *Turn to the **next page**.*

The sound startles you to attention, and you grab the receiver and snap "Hello!"

"Ouch! What are you so mad at?" an unfamiliar male voice asks.

"Myself," you grumble.

"Cheer up. Whatever's wrong can't be that bad."

"It's worse than bad," you gripe. Suddenly you realize you don't know who you're talking to. "Who is this, anyway?"

"Alex Reed-Cohen."

"Alex who?" you question, trying to place the name.

"Reed-Cohen."

"I don't think I know you."

"Well, I go to Ross Academy, and I work part-time for my parents' business. I like cars, dogs, and pizza. Does that answer your question?"

You stare at the phone and shake your head in bewilderment. "Who *are* you?"

"I thought we already established that," he teases. "I'm Alex Reed—"

"I got the name. But what are you calling for? *Who* are you calling for?"

*Turn to the **next page**.*

He laughs. "Actually, I was calling to order a pizza. A large combination, hold the olives. Guess I got the wrong number."

You giggle. "You guessed right."

"So a large pizza is out of the question?" he jokes.

"Absolutely."

"What about a date?"

"A date!" you exclaim. "But I don't know you."

"And I don't know you. A match made in telephone heaven." Alex continues, "I'll level with you. See, I've been invited to this great party on Saturday at the Changs. And I could really use a—"

"Did you say Chang? As in Emilee Chang?"

"Yeah. Do you know her?"

"Do I!" you exclaim. "I've been invited to Emilee's party, too."

"This is fate! You've got to go with me now. What do you say?" Alex asks.

If you want to go out with Alex,
*turn to the **next page**.*

If you don't want to go out with Alex,
*turn to **page 82**.*

"This is really crazy," you say. "But yes. I'll go out with you."

He whoops triumphantly. "Terrific! What time do you want me to pick you up?"

"I'd rather meet you at Emilee's house."

"Okay. But how will we know each other?"

You describe yourself and tell him your name. Then you ask him what he looks like.

"What if I say I'm tall, dark, and handsome?"

"I'd think you were lying."

"And you'd be right. My hair is light brown, not dark. I'll never be over six feet, but I'm not exactly short either. And handsome? Well, I resemble my brother and he's nice looking."

"Maybe I should go out with your brother," you tease.

"If Alan finds out I'm going to the Chang mansion with a date, he'll want to go just to see who it is. But forget it. You're with me."

"Sounds like fun."

"So I'll see you tomorrow night?"

"It's a date," you say, and you think to yourself, a *mystery* date!

 *Turn to page 46.*

♥ "No, I'm sorry," Timothy shakes his head. You smile with relief. "My dances are all reserved for the prettiest girl in the room."

Then Timothy leans down and kisses you right in the middle of the dance floor.

You love it as much as you thought you would. In fact, you don't even notice as Tara Lee furiously stomps back to Nathan.

The band starts up a slow, romantic melody.

The kiss ends and you smile into Timothy's sweet, hazel eyes. You take his hand and say, "Come on, Mr. MTV. Let's dance."

The End

♥ On the way to the soda bar, you see a too-familiar face. "Nathan!" you exclaim.

His gaze locks with yours and he says bluntly, "I need to talk to you."

You can't answer. Just being near Nathan has stolen your breath and sped up your heart. You want to sob out loud because you can no longer hide from the truth. You still care about Nathan.

"Will you listen to me?" Nathan asks.

"I don't know. . . ."

Timothy frowns at Nathan. "Back off. She's with me tonight."

"Please go away, Nathan," you say.

"But we need to talk."

"I have nothing to say to you. Timothy is my date. And Tara Lee is yours."

"Tara Lee isn't special like you," Nathan says softly. "I really messed up and I'm sorry. Give me another chance."

How often you've dreamed of hearing these words from Nathan. But now it's too late.

 *Turn to the **next page**.*

"Timothy is my date," you say firmly, as your heart breaks into micro-pieces.

"Give me just ten minutes," Nathan begs you.

"No."

"Then five minutes," he pleads. "How about a quick dance? We always made a great couple on the dance floor."

"That's in the past."

"But it could be in the future."

"Not anymore. Nathan, it's over. We're seeing other people, just as you wanted."

"But you're my girl and you still love me. I can tell you do."

Timothy looks deeply into your face and asks quietly, "Is this true?"

 *Turn to the **next page**.*

"I don't know. Maybe." You're tired of fighting your feelings.

Timothy looks away and sighs. He then turns to you and says, "I don't want to stand in your way."

"You aren't," you tell him.

"I'm not so sure about that," Timothy says sadly. "Go ahead and talk with Nathan. Find out the truth."

You start to argue, but your gaze falls on Nathan and old feelings and memories overwhelm you.

Timothy's right.

It's time to find out the truth. Do you still love Nathan enough to trust him with your heart one more time?

*Turn to the **next page**.*

Wordlessly, you follow Nathan out of the room, down a narrow hallway, and into a quiet book-lined room.

"No place more private than a library," Nathan says, his lips curving in that familiar, charming smile you love to see.

"So, talk," you say coolly.

"Still mad at me?"

"Shouldn't I be? You're the one who decided we should see other people."

"I blew it. I'm sorry."

"Being sorry isn't enough," you retort. You remember how deeply Nathan hurt you, and you're afraid he'll hurt you again.

He gently touches your arm and says in a low, sincere voice, "I've missed you."

Melting into his arms is tempting. But you turn around and stare at the bookshelves, instead. Your eyes dart from encyclopedias to leather-bound classics to titles with odd foreign names.

"So dull old books are more interesting than I am?" Nathan jokes, coming up beside you.

 *Turn to the next page.*

"I don't know right now," you say, turning to him. "Your date with Tara Lee might have bombed, but I was having fun with Timothy."

"Would you rather be with Timothy?"

"No," you answer honestly. "I still care about you."

"I knew it!" he cries.

"But caring about you doesn't mean I want to be your girlfriend again." You take a deep breath and add in a pained voice, "You really hurt me, Nathan. And seeing you with Tara Lee tonight . . . well, I don't know if things can ever be the same between us."

His fingers grasp yours firmly and you stare into his gentle eyes. If only you could forgive and forget. But this has all happened so quickly. And while you're struggling with your feelings for Nathan, you're also worried about Timothy. You feel like a creep for leaving him. After all, he's not only your date, but he's a good friend, too.

Why does love have to be so complicated?

Suddenly the library door bursts open.

*Turn to the **next page**.*

A kid in a clown suit with a blue-and-green wig on bellows out a laugh and stomps one huge duck-shaped foot against the carpet. "Enough lovey-dovey junk! It's game time!"

You stare in astonishment. A clown? Then you recognize him.

"Oh, hi, Chad. Love your costume!" you say, laughing. Chad Estaban is in your English class. He's the school cut-up and is very fun to be around. His timing, though, isn't always the best.

Chad chuckles. "Hey, guys, c'mon. Emilee has some great games planned for everyone in the main room."

"We're kind of busy right now," Nathan says.

Chad waves his hands as he walks out the door. "No excuses. Come on!"

"Maybe we should go," you tell Nathan.

"But nothing's settled between us."

"I need time to think, anyway," you say. "Might as well see what games Emilee has planned."

"Okay." He shrugs. "But no one's getting me to play musical chairs or pin-the-tail-on-the-donkey!"

 *Turn to the **next** page.*

Minutes later, you squeeze in the back of a large rowdy crowd. The music is deafening. Laughter is directed at something going on at the center of the dance floor. Nathan guides you closer to the action. At last you can see.

Emilee is standing onstage with Tyler, judging a dancing contest. Six couples are dancing wildly to the cheering of the crowd.

"Tara Lee's out there," Nathan says, his face near yours so you can hear.

"So is Timothy!" you add in astonishment. You recognize his partner, Jennifer Wells, from school.

No wonder Timothy was so eager to dance. He's fantastic! Where in the world did he learn to move like that? And why didn't Lori tell you?

The contest continues, and you watch in fascination. One couple, then another is eliminated. Third to be cut out are Tara Lee and her muscled partner. Two couples remain, and you're rooting for Timothy and Jennifer. They just have to win!

Turn to page 55.

28

♥ "Bill, how could you!" someone shouts.

You recognize Lori's voice. She's standing in the doorway and her hazel eyes are blazing.

"Lori!" Bill chokes, leaving you and rushing over to his girlfriend. "Thank goodness you're here. Your so-called best friend was coming on to me."

"Me? Coming on to *you*?" you gasp.

"Don't deny it," Bill says. "You were all over me the minute Lori was out of sight. Not that I'm surprised. You've been hot for me for ages."

Lori glares at Bill. "Shut up. You're so full of lies, you make me sick."

"But babe," Bill says softly. "You're my girl."

Lori pushes him away. "Not anymore. And don't call me 'babe.'"

Bill stares hard at Lori, seems to realize he's lost this war, then shrugs and slinks off the patio.

When he's gone, Lori sinks into a chair. Her eyes are moist and her face is pale.

"I can't believe he could do that," she moans.

Turn to page 50.

♥ "You mean I have to bring a date?" You twist the phone cord around your fingers anxiously. "But I don't have a boyfriend."

"Too bad you broke up with Nathan last week," Lori says sympathetically. She's dating Bill Sweeney, so she doesn't have to worry about who she'll take.

"You know that Nathan and I were getting too serious," you say. Deep down you know it was more Nathan's idea than yours to break up. After all, it was his idea to see other people. You haven't had any interest in anyone but him.

"I hear he's seeing Tara Lee Tracy."

"Tara Lee!" you gasp. You and Nathan went out for three months, and it hurts to know he's interested in snobby Tara Lee. "If Nathan shows up with Tara Lee at the party, I've *got* to have a date!" you say with a slight panic in your voice.

"You could ask my brother," Lori suggests.

"Timothy? Are you kidding?" you exclaim.

"Tim is smart and really nice. Plus he's older than us. Why not give him a chance?"

You tell Lori you'll think about it and hang up. You flop down on your bed and stare up at the ceiling.

*If you decide to ask Timothy to the party, turn to **page 103**.*

*If you decide not to ask Timothy to the party, turn to **page 83**.*

30

A five-member band plays loud music, and groups of kids are everywhere. Some lounge on couches, some dance under a canopy of little colored lights, and others talk excitedly in small groups.

You spot Emilee Chang on the dance floor. She's striking in snug black knit leggings and a sophisticated blazer, with just the right amount of shiny gold jewelry. She's swaying to the beat with her handsome dark-haired boyfriend, Tyler.

"Want to say hi to Emilee?" Lori asks.

You shake your head. "Maybe later. She's busy now."

Lori raises her eyebrows knowingly. "Yeah. You're right. And that's my kind of busy." Lori grabs Bill by the arm. "Come on. Let's dance."

You wave as Lori and her beau join the other happy couples on the dance floor. You'd like to dance, too, and wish you had a date of your own. But no such luck.

You wander to the soda bar and order a cherry cola.

You turn to see Jennifer Wells from your school. You don't know her well, but you've always thought she seemed nice. She's very smart, but so quiet that few kids notice her. Tonight she's wearing a soft flower print outfit that complements her pale blond hair.

"Hi, Jennifer. How's it going?"

"Great for everyone else. But I don't have a date, so I'm feeling out of place."

Turn to page 91.

♥ "Hi, Chad," you say nervously.

Chad turns and a big smile lights up his face. "Hi! You're just the person I need."

"Need?"

He grabs your hand and leads you down the middle of the mall. "I need a female's opinion." He pulls you inside a wig shop.

"Wigs?" you say in amazement.

Chad laughs and fits a green-and-blue wig over his dark hair. "How does this look?"

"Ridiculous. I prefer your natural hair," you answer, giggling. This is all kind of weird, and you wonder if Chad is date material after all.

He takes off the wig and pushes his hand through his hair. He explains that he's buying a wig for a clown costume. You wonder why he wants a clown costume, but you don't ask. You have something more important to discuss with Chad.

"Uh, Chad. I got an invitation to Emilee's party."

"Me, too!" he says, paying for the colorful wig and walking with you back into the mall.

Relieved, you smile at Chad. "Are you going?"

"Sure. If I can find a date."

You take a deep breath. "How about me?"

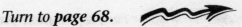

*Turn to **page 68.***

♥ "No," you say, switching the receiver to your other ear. "Let's go straight to the party. I don't want to miss out on anything."

There's a long pause on the other end of the phone. Finally Chad says, "I guess this party means a lot to you."

"I'm excited that Emilee invited me," you admit.

"Fine," he says in a flat tone. "I'll pick you up around six."

X O X O X

As you climb into Chad's car on Saturday night, you ask, "Why is your clown costume in the backseat?"

He shrugs. "No special reason."

You notice an edge to Chad's tone. "Is anything wrong?" you ask, studying his face. You decided to wear your favorite, most flattering purple dress, and Chad hasn't said a word about it. What's his problem?

"Nothing is wrong!" he snaps.

For the rest of the ride neither of you says a word. Chad seems hostile and tense. If he doesn't cheer up soon, this date is going to be a major pain.

Could the clown suit have anything to do with Chad's black mood?

 *Turn to the **next page**.*

At the party, Chad's sour mood continues. The live band is really good and the dance floor is crammed with happy couples. Except for you and Chad.

He sips on a lemon soda and stares off into space. He's a walking bad attitude if you ever saw one. You try to lure him out on to the dance floor, but he says he's too tired.

"Tired?" you complain. "But we just got here! What is with you tonight?"

His eyes narrow and he answers, "Nothing."

"I don't believe it."

"I just keep thinking about a friend of mine. I really should have visited him tonight."

"What friend?"

"You wouldn't understand."

"Give me a chance."

"I already did." He puts his glass down on a tray and turns. "If I'm going to be at this party, I might as well have fun. My kind of fun."

Then Chad whirls off, and you're left standing alone.

 *Turn to the **next page**.*

You order a cherry cola from the soda bar and slump down into a chair.

You realize that not letting Chad make his mysterious stop was a bad move. And now you'll never have another chance with him.

Several minutes later, a wigged clown bursts into the party.

You recognize the bright wig.

"Chad!" you cry, but he walks right past you.

He sweeps over to Emilee Chang and dramatically presents her with a pretty bouquet of balloons.

Chad wows everyone with magic tricks, silly dance routines, and funny charades.

For the rest of the evening, Chad is the life of the party, and you are left all alone.

The End

♥ You and Lori walk into the pool area and see two dark figures embracing.

"Bill Sweeney!" Lori exclaims.

"Lori! This isn't what it looks like," Bill says, dropping his hands from Tara Lee's waist.

Lori glares at Bill. "Don't bother lying. I know you were kissing Tara Lee."

"Is it my fault she can't keep her hands off me?"

You want to puke at Bill's lies.

Tara Lee smooths her long black hair and sweeps past Lori and Bill. "It was fun while it lasted, but I can't handle scenes. I'm out of here."

You put your hand gently on Lori's arm. "Let's go."

Bill pleads, "Lori, stay with me. You're the only girl for me. I'm crazy about you."

"Then why did you sneak off with Tara Lee?"

"She tricked me into coming in here with her. I'm sorry, Lori. Forgive me."

"No way!" Lori whirls on Bill. "If you want Tara Lee, that's fine with me."

"I don't want her," he insists, pleading with Lori. "She's nothing to me."

"And you're nothing to me!" Lori turns around, gesturing for you to follow her. "Come on. If I stay any longer, I'll lose my temper and push him in the pool."

 *Turn to the **next page.***

You smile at the image of Bill floundering in the star-shaped pool. It would serve the creep right!

But Lori controls her temper. You leave the noisy party and find a quiet patio.

Lori sinks into a wicker chair. "Bill and I are through forever."

You pat her shoulder. "He isn't good enough for you."

"Maybe. I just wish breaking up didn't hurt so much."

You nod sympathetically, remembering how great it was to be with Nathan, and how painful it was to see him with Tara Lee.

Lori tucks a piece of hair behind her ear and manages a smile. "Guess the biggest problem now is how to get home from this party."

"Oops!" you cry. "I forgot that Bill drove us."

Turn to page 66.

❤ You borrow your parents' station wagon and drive to the mall.

Shopping is one of your favorite activities. Walking past store after store, you stop and peer into the window of Pet Jamboree, where a litter of Yorkshire puppies is on display. You could spend hours window-shopping, but you get down to business and enter Bodacious Boutique.

You gasp when you see the salesclerk. Her black hair reaches to her waist and her makeup is perfect, of course. It's Tara Lee Tracy.

"Well, hello there. This is sure a surprise," Tara Lee says in a soft Southern voice.

"Hi," you say weakly. Chatting with your old boyfriend's new girlfriend is not exactly your idea of fun.

She smiles sweetly. "May I help you with something?"

You shake your head. "No, thanks. I'll look around myself."

"Looking for something special?" Tara Lee asks.

"Yeah," you admit. "Something for a party."

Her green eyes glitter. "Don't tell me *you're* invited to Emilee's, too?"

You can't resist smiling. "Okay. I won't tell you."

*Turn to the **next** page.*

"You *are* going!" Tara Lee declares. "I'm going, too, and you'll never guess who my date is."

"Oh, let me try," you say dryly. "Nathan Fields?"

"That's right! You must be a mind reader. And Nathan is just the perfect date. He's so cute and considerate." She smirks at you. "But then you already knew that. I can't imagine why you let him get away."

"Some might say that he let *me* get away," you reply. Inside, you're steaming. How can Nathan be attracted to such a fluff-brain?

"Emilee was in here a couple of days ago, too. Of course, she could buy the whole store if she wanted," Tara Lee says, with a hint of jealousy in her voice. Then she peers at you coyly and asks, "So, do you have a date for Emilee's party yet?"

> ## BUT WAIT!
>
> ### Do you want to change your mind?
>
> *Are you having second thoughts about going to a party with your best friend's brother? If you wish you hadn't asked Timothy out, turn to page 83.*

"Yeah."

"Oh, really?" She sounds surprised.

"Sure. My date is even more perfect than Nathan."

"Who?"

"You'll find out at the party," you say mysteriously, turning your back on Tara Lee.

  *Turn to the **next page**.*

You forget about Tara Lee and Nathan while you sort through racks of clothes. You find three possible outfits: a pleated red skirt with a red-and-white blouse, a blue miniskirt and sweater, and a long blazer with a great pair of black leggings. Any one of these would look fantastic, so you take all three into the dressing room.

You try on the pleated skirt and blouse and study your reflection in the mirror. Too much red.

You try on the blue miniskirt and sweater. The color is flattering and the sweater feels great. Your eyes sparkle with delight. You know you look terrific.

You try on the leggings and blazer and once again stare at your reflection. You look older and sophisticated.

Tara Lee comes up behind you and comments, "Very nice choice. I'd take it if I were you. It's perfect for Emilee's party."

"But it makes my face look pale," you say.

"A bit of makeup will fix that right up. It's a dynamite combo. Very chic."

"Are you sure?" You worry about fitting in with Emilee's crowd.

"Trust me," Tara Lee says in a cozy, confidential tone, as if the two of you were great pals. "Blue is boring. If you want to impress Emilee, go with the black one."

You think over Tara Lee's advice while you change back into your regular clothes. If she's so positive about the black leggings and blazer, there's only one choice you can make.

 *Turn to the **next page**.*

You walk up to the cash register and drape your choice on the counter.

"This isn't black!" Tara Lee complains.

You smile sweetly. "I decided to go with blue. Even if it is boring."

She glares at you, but doesn't say anything while she rings up your purchase. As you leave the store, you hug the bag to your chest. Tara Lee may have Nathan, but you have a fantastic new outfit, and you can't wait to show it off at Emilee's party!

X O X O X

Saturday arrives, and you're ready for a thrilling evening. You've spent an hour getting ready. Your new clothes look great, and you feel like Cinderella waiting for Prince Charming to escort her to the ball. You just hope that Timothy turns out to be a "princely" date!

At five o'clock the phone rings. It's Timothy. "There's . . . there's a little problem. My car isn't working too well. I was wondering if you'd mind going in my dad's pickup."

"Pickup?" You shudder at the image of Mr. Cramer's beat-up old truck. You had looked forward to riding in Timothy's mint green sports car.

"Well," Timothy persists, "do you mind if we go in the pickup?"

If you agree to go in the gray pickup,
*turn to **page 58.***

*If you insist on going in the sports car, turn to **page 53.***

 "And I'm Alex," another voice says.

You turn and blink in amazement. Alex is behind you *and* in front of you. You're seeing double!

"Twins?" you murmur, sinking down into a chair.

Alex and Alan grin.

"You caught us," Alan says, reaching for Jennifer's hand. He continues. "This was all Alex's idea. He knew how much I wanted to see the inside of this mansion. I'm an art fanatic and I've heard about the Chang art collection. I just had to see it for myself."

Alex adds, "But I was the one invited to this party. So Alan hid in the back of the van and slipped into the party when no one was looking. We figured everyone would assume he was me."

"Which is exactly what happened," you say. "It was a dumb idea."

Jennifer smiles at Alan. "Maybe not such a dumb idea. Otherwise we never would have met."

"I agree," Alan says, looking shyly at Jennifer.

"So, which of you *really* hurt your ankle?" you ask.

"This one is all yours, Alan," Alex says. He's clearly looking forward to whatever Alan has to say.

Alan turns to you sheepishly. "Well, I . . . I kind of lied about the ankle. I'm really sorry—I was afraid Alex would see us together, and then I'd be busted bigtime."

"I understand. I'm just glad it wasn't what I thought it was," you say, smiling at Alex. Alan and Jennifer wander back to the dance floor.

And you're alone with Alex—the *real* Alex.

*Turn to **page 100**.*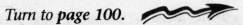

♥ You grin at Jennifer. "You're right. No reason to miss a terrific evening." You and Jennifer return to the party.

Emilee is standing by a refreshment table, talking with a young woman in a maid's uniform. Emilee waves to Jennifer. "There you are. I wondered where you disappeared to."

"Hi, Emilee," Jennifer says. "We've been enjoying some girl talk by the pool."

"And you didn't invite me?" Emilee teases, including you in her friendly smile.

"Next time," Jennifer promises. "Right now we're in a dancing mood."

Emilee moans. "Not me. My shoes are squeezing the life force out of my toes, but Tyler could dance all night. Jen, want to do me a big favor and dance with my date for a while?"

Jennifer blushes. "Me? With Tyler? Won't he mind?"

Emilee laughs. "Tyler expects to dance all night. He thinks I'm a wimp because my feet ache." She rolls her eyes and makes a face. "Guys just don't understand the agony we go through for them."

You all giggle. You're pleasantly surprised that Emilee and Jennifer are such fun girls. Even if you never dance a step tonight, getting to know them better has made this a great Saturday night.

*Turn to the **next** page.*

Jennifer goes off to dance with Tyler, and you stand beside Emilee. The blaring rock music makes you itch to dance, but you don't see any available guys.

The one guy you do see is Nathan. It's hard not to stare at him as he sits next to Tara Lee on a couch. Tara Lee's raven black head rests against Nathan's blond one, and it's like your heart is being squeezed. It makes no sense. You shouldn't care. And yet you do. . . .

"Are you all right?" Emilee asks gently. Her gaze follows yours, and she nods as if she understands.

"I shouldn't have come without a date. I'd better go home."

"You're staying here," Emilee says firmly. "No date? Why didn't you say something? I can fix you up with a super date. Tyler's cousin D.J. doesn't have a date, either."

"Tyler's cousin?" you ask.

She flips her dark hair over her shoulder and grins. "You'll adore him. He's around here somewhere—maybe in the billiards room. Stay put while I go look for him."

You stand there, but you're afraid to meet D.J. He's probably not your type. Tyler seems nice, but his cousin might be a total geek or a boring snob. Besides, your heart is breaking because of Nathan. You don't need any more romantic complications.

Cousin D.J. can find some other girl. You're going home!

 *Turn to the **next page**.*

You leave the room and walk down a long hallway to the front door. What timing! A couple of girls from your neighborhood are leaving, too.

"Hey, Jackie. Hi, Jessica," you say. "Do you mind if I catch a ride home with you two?"

"Of course not!" Jessica replies. "Jackie's driving her parents' Cadillac!"

The three of you hop into the large gorgeous car and head home.

"Jackie, did you meet Tyler's adorable cousin?" Jessica asks, searching for a good song on the radio.

"He's adorable?" you ask. Suddenly you're not so sure you did the right thing, running out so fast.

"Yes, I met him, and yes, he *is* adorable! I loved his glasses and his dark hair," Jackie coos. "I made Tyler promise to set me up with Devin when he's back in town."

"Devin? With round tortoiseshell glasses?" Now you *know* you shouldn't have run out of Emilee's party.

"That's the one!" Jackie says. She turns to you. "Did you meet him?"

"I bumped into him once," you say quietly, as the realization sinks in that you blew it not once, but twice with your dream guy.

The End

♥ You're glad you decided to go with Lori and Bill to the party . . . without a date.

"Two gorgeous girls just for me," Bill says, opening the back door of his car. Lori is already sitting in front, and Bill climbs in and drapes an arm around her shoulders. "Let's get movin'. It's party time!"

The words "party time" echo in your head. You cross your fingers and hope tonight turns out to be wonderful.

Emilee's house is impressive. Bill drives through the massive gates and up a curvy tree-lined road. The car stops in front of the white pillared three-story mansion and a parking attendant greets you.

"Welcome to the Chang estate," the attendant says, opening your car door. You feel like a movie star as you walk up the marble steps and enter Emilee's fabulous home.

A butler leads you through a tiled entryway and down a carpeted hallway. You admire framed portraits, crystal chandeliers, and unusual art pieces.

"This way, please," the butler says.

You hold your breath in eager anticipation.

At last, you're at the party!

 *Turn to page 30.*

♥ It's Saturday night, 6:40 P.M., and you're ready for the bash. You've looked at your watch a million times, anxious for the evening to get started. You glance in the mirror and wonder what Alex will think.

You catch a ride to the party with Lori and Bill. As you and Lori talk about who will be there, inside you're hoping it won't take too long to find Alex. When you see Emilee's mansion, you gaze in astonishment. It looks more like a palace than someone's house. As a parking attendant takes Bill's car, you notice a white van pulling up. On the side of the van are elaborate paintings of cakes and bridal gowns, along with the words "Reed-Cohen Wedding Specialists."

Reed-Cohen! So the driver must be Alex! You watch out of the corner of your eye as the driver steps out of the van. He's just the right height, not too short or too tall. You immediately have the urge to touch his shiny light-brown hair where it curls around his ears. You like his large hazel eyes and his nice, full mouth—a mouth that you might kiss at the end of the evening!

 *Turn to the **next page.***

You tell Lori and Bill to go ahead, and you wait for Alex to get to the foot of the marble steps.

"Alex?" you ask tentatively. He smiles.

"Pizza girl?" he asks right back. You smile.

Then Alex offers you his arm as he escorts you up the steps into the Chang mansion.

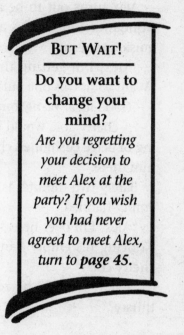

But Wait!

Do you want to change your mind?

Are you regretting your decision to meet Alex at the party? If you wish you had never agreed to meet Alex, turn to page 45.

"What's a wedding specialist?" you ask, trying to make small talk as Alex opens the door.

"My family plans weddings. Mom handles the cakes, gown, and invitations. My dad oversees transportation, decorations, and floral arrangements. My brother Alan and I help out when we can. Since Alan is the family artist, he painted the van's logo."

"And what do you do?"

"Answer phones and run errands. I'm really into cars, so driving the van is my job. And I like it."

"Sounds like fun."

"It is. But this," he says, pointing to the live band, "really sounds like fun!"

 *Turn to the next page.*

You spot Lori and Bill snuggling to a slow song on the raised wooden dance floor. A five-member band plays, and colored lights shine on the dancers as you and Alex make your way to the dance floor.

Alex turns out to be a great dancer, and you have a wonderful time in his arms. After several dances, the music speeds up.

"Alex, I'm getting tired," you yell over the music. "Want to sit this one out?"

"Good idea. Want something to drink?"

"A cherry cola would be great." You point to a grouping of beige cushioned chairs and tell Alex you'll wait for him there.

Barely two minutes later, you see Alex walk past you, empty-handed.

"Alex, I'm over here," you say with an amused smile. Noticing his empty hands, you ask, "Didn't they have cherry cola?"

"Cherry cola?" he repeats as if puzzled. "Are you thirsty?"

 *Turn to the **next page.***

"You know I am. Are you always such a tease?"

Alex smiles and glances away for a second. "Not always," he says, widening his smile. "Only when I'm with a pretty girl."

"Yeah, right," you reply, blushing.

"It's the truth. I enjoy lovely things . . . and people. Beauty like yours belongs on a canvas."

What a romantic comment! you think happily. You're too flattered to speak. You're really impressed by this side of Alex.

"Let me go get you that cherry cola," Alex says. "I'll be back before you can say Pablo Picasso!"

You nod, surprised by Alex's quick mood changes. From a rowdy dancer to a playful tease to a romantic poet. He's definitely a complex guy—and you look forward to learning everything about him.

You just might be falling for this guy you met through the phone lines.

 *Turn to page 119.*

♥ "You'll find a nice guy you can really trust," you say, sitting down next to Lori and putting your arm around her shoulders.

Lori wipes her eyes and gives you a curious glance. "Where's your date?"

"Chad's being a real Bozo, and I wasn't into playing clown all night."

"Oh, no," Lori sympathizes. "Aren't we a sad pair? But even worse, who will drive us home now?"

Emilee Chang peeks her head through the open doorway. "Did I hear someone say they needed a ride?"

You and Lori nod and explain what's happened.

"Guys can be real jerks," Emilee says with feeling. "My friend Jennifer couldn't get a date tonight and she's bored. And my own guy, Tyler, has been bossing me around all night, and I'm tired of it."

"We shouldn't let guys run our lives," Lori states.

"Who needs them, anyway?" you add.

"Not us, that's for sure," Lori says firmly.

A mischievous light glimmers in Emilee's eyes, and she snaps her fingers. "You two just gave me a fantastic idea. You're right, we don't need guys. Follow me."

 *Turn to the **next page**.*

Emilee leads you to a large room with a Jacuzzi and star-shaped pool.

"The party can go on without me for a while," Emilee says. "We can relax in here. While I go dig up some swimsuits, can you go find Jennifer and see if she wants to join us?"

"Sure," you say. "We girls need to stick together."

"You bet," Lori replies. She kicks off one shoe and wiggles her toes in the foamy, warm Jacuzzi. "The water is heavenly! I love hot tubs."

You nod enthusiastically. "This is a fantastic idea!"

Emilee grins. "And you know what the best part is?"

You and Lori exchange glances. Giggling, you answer at the same time, "No boys!"

The End

♥ "But you said you liked romantic guys—which means Alan, not me. So I decided if you preferred Alan, then I'd let you have him. Even though I hate to think of the two of you together." He pauses and adds sincerely, "I really like you."

You tug on his hand and pull him next to you. "And I like you, too. Alex found me over the phone, not Alan."

"You wouldn't rather be with my brother?" Alex asks sincerely.

"Not a chance. I don't need romantic words. Actions say more than words."

His hazel eyes sparkle with mischief. "Here's some action."

He leans close to you and gives you a sweet, wonderful kiss.

When the kiss is over, you smile at your dream date and say softly, "Now, that's romance."

The End

♥ "I'd really rather go in the sports car," you say.

"Are you sure?"

"Definitely. Your car is so awesome. I've always wanted to ride in it."

"You have?" Timothy sounds pleased. "Well . . . okay. It's just that my engine's been sounding strange."

"I don't mind a little noise," you assure him.

"Okay. I'll be there soon."

"I'll be waiting," you say. Then you hang up.

You hum a cheerful melody and practically dance over to the mirror. Your makeup is just right, and you look great in the blue outfit. You predict that tonight will be the best night of your entire life.

An hour later, there's a knock on the front door.

You open the door and Timothy is standing there with a single pink rose in his hand.

"For you," he says, handing you the rose.

"How sweet. Thanks, Timothy."

*Turn to the **next page**.*

As you smell the fragrant flower, Timothy stares at you in obvious admiration. Your heart fills with pleasure. This is a side of Timothy you've never seen. He's not only smart and considerate, but very romantic, too.

You take a few moments to put the rose in a vase, then step outside with Timothy. The green sports car shines under the streetlights. You secretly hope Nathan notices you arriving at the party in this cool car.

And to think Timothy wanted to go in a beat-up old truck! Good thing you had the sense to say no way.

Timothy opens the passenger door and offers you a hand into the car. You fasten your seatbelt and smooth away the creases in your skirt.

"Are you comfortable?" Timothy asks as he revs up the engine. The car roars fiercely. It sounds good to you. Timothy must have been worrying for nothing.

You lean back in your seat. "This is perfect."

Timothy pauses for a red light and smiles at you. Your heart speeds up and you wonder for the first time what it would be like to kiss him. You hope you find out.

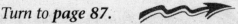
*Turn to **page 87**.*

♥ The music stops and Emilee flashes a dazzling smile. "And the winners are . . . Timothy Cramer and Jennifer Wells!"

Applause shakes the room, and you wrap your arms around Nathan. He returns the embrace, and suddenly you realize this is no longer about Timothy's success. It feels good to be next to Nathan, although you're still afraid. What if you start dating and he decides to dump you again?

You pull away.

"Don't run away. Let's finish talking," Nathan says.

You hesitate, trying to listen to your heart and your head at the same time. Both are giving separate messages. Which is the right one?

Emilee is now announcing a new contest.

"Grab your sweetheart and get ready for the sweetest contest of the night," Emilee shouts.

Nathan says, "I'm not in the mood for a contest. I need to know where we stand."

"Can't it wait till later?" you ask, stalling for time.

"I don't think so. We need to settle this now," he insists.

You stare into his eyes, loving every curve of his face and wanting to trust him. What will you do?

*If you talk with Nathan, turn to the **next page**.*

If you enter Emilee's "sweet" contest, turn to page 110.

"Okay, Nathan," you agree. "I guess this isn't the time for fun and games."

Nathan leads you to the back of the room and orders two colas from the soda bar. You find a wicker loveseat outside on the quiet patio and sit beside him.

As you sip your drink, you gaze fondly at Nathan. You're sure you'll never care for another boy the way you care for him. But caring means putting yourself at risk of heartbreak, and that terrifies you.

Nathan caresses your hair and asks softly, "So, will you be my girlfriend?"

"What about Tara Lee?"

"As far as I'm concerned, she's history. I need a girl who can talk about more than malls and shoe sales. Now what about your date?"

"Timothy's a great pal. We've been friends so long, I don't think we could be anything else."

"So does this mean I have a chance?" Nathan asks hopefully.

*If your answer is yes, turn to **page 101.***

If your answer is no, turn to the next page.

There's no more stalling for time.

You take a deep breath and shake your head. "No. Nathan, I just can't do it."

"But you said you cared about me."

"I do," you admit, wiping a tear from your cheek. "I'll never forget you. But I can't forgive you, either."

"You're blowing it," he says quietly. "We could have been great together."

"I know," you whisper sadly. "I hope I'm not making the biggest mistake of my life. Good-bye, Nathan."

X O X O X

Twenty years later, you're bitter, lonely, and living alone.

Nathan is happily married, the father of three terrific kids, and a famous soap opera star.

Nathan was the love of your life, and you finally realize that not forgiving him was a *big* mistake!

The End

♥ "No, I don't mind if we take your dad's truck," you say, hoping Timothy doesn't think you're disappointed. After all, you still have a date to Emilee's party, and you're really looking forward to seeing how the evening will turn out.

You hear Timothy's relieved sigh over the phone. "That's great. I was really worried for a minute. I mean, not all girls would be so understanding."

"Well, I'm not 'all girls.' I'm just me."

"I'm glad," he says.

Your heart speeds up, and you suddenly feel awkward talking to Timothy. You grip the receiver a bit too tightly and try to lighten the moment. "Hey, we're wasting time yakking on the phone. I'm ready to party."

"I get the hint." He chuckles. "I'll be there soon."

"I'll be waiting."

An hour later, sounds of a truck backfiring tell you Timothy has arrived.

*Turn to the **next** page.*

The doorbell rings, and you slowly open the door.

Timothy looks at his feet, smiles shyly, and holds out a single pink rose. "For you."

You return the smile, bring the flower to your face, and inhale. Sweet, soft, and fragrant. "Thanks, Timothy. It's beautiful."

"So are you."

Three words from the boy you've known since kindergarten turn you to mush. Your head spins and your breath catches. You feel wonderful!

You take a few moments to put the rose in a vase, then step outside with Timothy.

*Turn to the **next page.***

The noisy, bumpy ride in Mr. Cramer's dented old pickup doesn't bother you one bit. You and Timothy gab about the past, like Lori's tenth birthday slumber party, when Timothy and his friends scared the girls so much that they all went home, except you.

Before you know it, you are driving through the massive iron gates of Emilee's home, then up a curvy tree-lined road. "Wow, this is some place," Timothy says.

"That's for sure," you agree, as the truck jerks to a stop in front of a white, pillared, three-story mansion.

A uniformed parking attendant greets you.

"May I park your vehicle for you?" he asks politely.

"Uh, sure," Timothy says.

"Be careful with this truck. Don't dent it," you jokingly tell the attendant, hoping to help Timothy relax.

It works. Timothy smiles and squeezes your hand.

As Timothy helps you out of the truck, you hear an approaching car. You turn and nearly faint when you see Nathan and Tara Lee pull up in a shiny red Corvette. Tara Lee's parents must have lent it to them for the evening.

 *Turn to the **next page.***

Your good mood dies a quick and painful death. You try to hurry Timothy inside, but he's talking to the attendant.

"No, no. Pump the pedal twice, *then* shift into first," Timothy says.

The engine makes a choking sound, then springs into life and rattles away.

Tara Lee steps out of the sports car and waves. "Interesting set of wheels," she says with a giggle.

You refuse to let Tara Lee annoy you. Instead of scowling, you just smile and wave, secretly wishing you could vanish into the ozone.

"Come on, Tara Lee," Nathan snaps. He glances uneasily at you, then turns away.

While another attendant hurries to take charge of the red Corvette, you walk with Timothy up marble stairs to the front door. Seeing Nathan again has stirred up painful memories, and it's not easy to ignore them.

Turn to page 124.

♥ Timothy shakes his head. "My car isn't going to explode. That's steam, not smoke."

"Steam? But what are we going to do?"

Timothy looks around. "We're a mile from a gas station. You can't stay here alone with the car. You'll have to walk to the station with me."

"In these shoes?" you cry.

He shrugs. "Or barefoot."

By the time you get to the gas station, you've ripped your skirt, stepped into a muddy puddle, and broken a shoe heel.

While Timothy makes towing arrangements with someone named Elmer, you wonder if you should have ridden in the pickup truck after all.

You never do make it to the Saturday night bash . . . nor do you find out what it's like to kiss Timothy.

The End

♥ You watch in growing anger as Tara Lee giggles at something Bill has whispered.

Suddenly the door is yanked open and light streams into the room. It's Nathan.

"Tara Lee, I've been looking for . . ."

Nathan's words trail off as he stares at Tara Lee and Bill. You can tell he's stunned to discover his girlfriend with another guy, and you feel sorry for him.

"Nathan!" Tara Lee shrieks. "I can explain."

Nathan walks over to Bill and Tara Lee. You've never seen such a cold look on Nathan's face, and you wonder what's going through his mind.

Nervously, Bill backs up to the pool's edge. "This is all very innocent, Nathan. I'd better be going."

Nathan says, "Not so fast, Bill. Stick around."

Tara Lee smooths her dark hair from her face and pouts, "Aren't you jealous, Natey?"

"Who? Me? No way. You and Bill make a great couple."

"We do?" Tara Lee says in a puzzled voice.

"Yup. I predict you two will go places together."

"Huh?" Tara Lee asks.

Nathan grins wickedly and lunges forward. He gives Bill a big push—right into the pool!

*Turn to the **next page**.*

Tara Lee reaches over to help Bill, but loses her balance and falls SPLAT! into the pool.

Nathan brushes his palms together, calm, confident, and content. Then he leaves.

Ignoring soggy Bill and Tara Lee, you jump up from your hiding place and hurry after Nathan. You check the main room, billiards room, library, and video arcade. Finally you spot Nathan in the hallway. He's headed outside.

"Nathan!" you call, running after him.

He stops and says, "I was just leaving."

You notice how his gaze softens as he looks at you. Does he still care? Is it possible?

"Nathan, you were great! Dunking Bill was really cool."

"How could you know about that?"

You smile mysteriously. "There's a lot I know."

He reaches out and lightly caresses your cheek. "Bet you don't know how much I've missed you. Seeing other people was a stupid idea."

"It was *your* stupid idea," you remind him.

"Tara Lee is an airhead. I had planned to break up with her after the party. Guess she beat me to it."

"But you had the last splash," you tease.

You both laugh and move toward each other. Your heart thumps wildly and you wonder what will happen next.

*Turn to the **next page**.*

A kiss is what happens next, and you hold on to Nathan as if he's the only boy in the world, which he is as far as you're concerned.

No kiss has ever been sweeter and so full of love. Being with Nathan feels so right.

When the kiss ends, you smile into Nathan's soft brown eyes. "Would you dance with me?"

He nods. "With you and only you."

You take his hand and head for the dance floor.

The party's been going on for hours, but for you it's only just begun.

At last, you've found your dream date.

The End

♥ "I'll call my parents," Lori suggests.

"Good idea," you say.

"You don't mind leaving early?" Lori asks.

"Nope. You can bet Tara Lee is back with Nathan, pretending to be wild about him. I don't feel like watching that scene all night."

"Or Tara Lee might be dancing with Bill," Lori guesses. "Either way, this party is ruined for both of us."

"Well," you say optimistically, "there's more to life than dating."

"Name one thing," Lori jokes.

"Triple chocolate ice cream and best friends."

"That's two things," she says, giggling. "But I agree. Ice cream and friends are the greatest."

Lori calls home, and soon her parents arrive to pick you both up.

You decide to have a mini-slumber party at Lori's house, and you spend the rest of the evening eating triple chocolate ice cream, watching old videos, and talking.

The next morning, you and your best friend hit the local art museum.

You decide that you'll survive just fine without boys . . . for now.

The End

♥ Reluctantly, you follow Timothy. He finds a spot on the packed floor and begins to move.

Timothy spins, slides, and sways to the beat. You mirror his moves, trying hard to keep up with him. He's *really* good, and you're totally amazed. There's nothing shy about Timothy when he's on the dance floor.

"Where did you learn to dance so well?" you ask, raising your voice so you can be heard over the thundering music.

He grins sheepishly. "When no one's around, I practice while watching MTV."

"Wow! MTV was a good teacher. I'm impressed. And I'm not the only one. Everyone's watching you."

"Not just me. They're watching us," he says, pulling you close to him. You're starting to wonder if he's going to kiss you . . . and you hope he will.

When the song's over, applause rings out in the room.

Suddenly Tara Lee appears and looks out from under her long dark lashes at Timothy. "That was great. You're the best dancer in the room. You just have to dance the next song with me."

Are you going to lose another boyfriend to this Southern cotton ball?

Turn to page 20.

68

♥ "That would be great!" Chad answers.

You feel so relieved. A simple question, a simple answer, and suddenly you have a date for Saturday night. You had no idea it could be so easy to ask a guy out.

You give Chad your address and phone number, and he promises to call you tonight.

You're so excited that you can't think about buying an outfit for the party. You're dying to tell Lori your good news.

When you phone her and tell her what's happened, she says in disbelief, "You have a date *already*?"

You twist the phone cord between your fingers and sigh happily. "Yeah, can you believe it? Chad is going to be the best date!"

"That's great. Hey, I've got an idea. Want to double date to the party? Bill can drive us all."

"That would be fun," you agree.

But that evening, when you discuss it on the phone with Chad, he says he can't.

"Why not?" you ask.

*Turn to the **next page**.*

"I need my own wheels . . . just in case."

"In case of what?" you ask, leaning against a pillow.

"I can't say. But if I can find what I'm looking for, I'll need to deliver it Saturday evening."

"What?" You wonder why he's being so mysterious.

"I'll tell you all about it on Saturday."

"Okay," you reply hesitantly.

"Relax," he says with a chuckle. "We're going to have a blast at the party. And that's a promise."

$$\times \quad \circ \quad \times \quad \circ \quad \times$$

On Saturday morning, Chad calls to ask a favor. He wants to pick you up early and stop somewhere before the party.

"Where?" you ask.

"The hospital," he says mysteriously.

"Are you sick?"

He laughs. "I'm not, but I want to visit a friend. Is it okay?"

*If you answer yes, turn to the **next page**.*

*If you answer no, turn to **page 32**.*

"I don't mind stopping by the hospital," you say. "As long as we're not too late for the party."

"No problem," he assures you.

He sounds confident, but you can't help but wonder if asking Chad to Emilee's party was the right thing to do.

X O X O X

On Saturday, the doorbell rings a few minutes before five o'clock. You scramble to brush your hair and dab on some lipstick.

When you open the door, instead of seeing Chad, you see a red-nosed, orange duck-footed, fuzzy-haired stranger.

Wait a minute…you recognize the green-and-blue wig.

"Chad?" you almost whisper. "Is that you?"

Bright painted lips widen into a goofy grin. "Sure is. How do I look?"

"Like a clown," you answer.

He laughs. "That's the idea."

Your mouth drops open. "But Emilee's bash isn't a costume party, so why are you dressed like that?"

*Turn to the **next page**.*

"To entertain and delight an audience."

"What audience? I don't understand. . . ."

"You will soon." He takes your hand in his oversized red glove and guides you to his car. You can't think of anything to say, so you wordlessly get into the car and hope the evening doesn't turn into a total disaster.

A short time later, Chad pulls into the parking lot in front of the city hospital.

"Are you checking into the mental ward?" you half-tease.

"You think I'm crazy?" he asks with a laugh.

"Certifiably. Most guys don't show up for dates in face paint and duck feet. Chad, what's going on?"

"We're going to the children's ward," he explains. "In my spare time, I perform for sick kids. One special kid needs me tonight, and I couldn't let him down. This won't take long. I promise."

"You visit sick kids?" you ask in amazement. Who would have thought wacky Chad did volunteer work? You asked him out because he's cute, and now you're learning about a whole other side to him.

When Chad struts into the children's ward, the kids go wild. They cheer, clap, and giggle. Even the sickest kids manage a big welcoming smile for Chad.

And your heart melts. You're totally impressed as Chad sings, jokes, and performs magic tricks for the kids.

*Turn to the **next page.***

Chad sits with a boy whose legs are in casts and suspended in midair. The boy looks about ten years old, and his face is sad.

"Hey, Ricky," Chad greets. "Where's your smile?"

"Lost it when I broke my legs," the boy says bitterly.

"Did you also lose this?" Chad asks, reaching into the air, snapping his fingers, and producing a rectangular card.

"Hey, that's a baseball card!" Ricky exclaims, his blue eyes lighting up with surprise.

Chad the clown chuckles. "Not just any card. Check it out."

"Wow! A Barry Bonds 1987 Fleer! I really need this card for my collection. Is it yours?"

"That depends," Chad says, scratching his fuzzy head.

"On what?" Ricky asks.

"If you can find your smile and work hard to get better, then it's yours. Is it a deal?"

Ricky grins as if he's won the lottery. "Sure thing! Thanks, Chad. You're the coolest clown in the world."

Chad nudges you and whispers, "Success! At least I have one fan."

"Make that two," you add warmly.

 *Turn to the **next page**.*

Chad glances at a wall clock and says, "Hey, if we're going to make it to Emilee's house, we should go."

"Wow," you say, "I had completely lost track of the time. I've been having so much fun with the kids."

Suddenly an idea pops into your head. Maybe you should skip the party and stay at the hospital.

*If you go to the bash, turn to **page 105.***

If you stay at the hospital, turn to the ***next page.***

You see how much Chad loves being with the kids, and you're having a wonderful time with Chad. You hadn't realized how incredible it makes you feel to help other people. You pull Chad aside and whisper, "Let's forget the party. We can have our own party here . . . with the kids."

His eyes widen. "You really mean that?"

"Yes. I've never met a guy who cared so much about other people. I'd rather stay and help you entertain the kids."

"But you're dressed for a party."

"And you're dressed for a circus," you tease. "We make an interesting pair, don't we?"

"A wonderful pair." He reaches out and caresses your cheek. "I'm glad you asked me out. You're the most incredible girl I've ever met."

You reach up and gently pull off his large red clown nose. He meets you halfway in a very sweet kiss. Soft, tender emotions fill you, and you feel very happy.

When the kiss is over, you tell Chad you want to be a clown, as you fit his red plastic nose over your own nose. Chad runs out to his car and comes back with a huge flowered hat and some denim overalls. Presto change-o! You're a clown.

*Turn to the **next page.***

You and Chad never make it to Emilee's party, but you don't mind. The two of you spend the evening clowning around in front of giggling kids. Chad teaches you a few card tricks to perform, and you're a hit! Your audience explodes with laughter and applause.

And this is only the beginning. . . .

Ten years later, you and Chad are happily married clowns with a traveling circus. You tour the world with your adorable triplet baby clowns, sharing fun, laughter, and love.

The End

♥ One more glance in the mirror and you decide to go with the purple tank dress. The color is perfect on you, and you've worn it only a few times, so it's practically new.

You have a dress, but now you need matching shoes. You wonder what shoes would go with violet purple. Your black sandals look okay, but they're a little scuffed. And your red shoes would clash.

You have no choice but to go shopping.

"Mom, may I borrow the car? I need to buy shoes for Emilee's party," you say, peeking into your mother's office. She works at home and you know she doesn't like to be disturbed, but this is important. Not exactly life-or-death drama, but close enough.

"Shoes? Sounds like a terrific idea. I could use a new pair of shoes, too."

"What?"

She smiles. "I need to pick up some running shoes, and I could use a break from paperwork, too. You don't mind if I join you, do you?"

 *Turn to the **next page**.*

You stare at your mother in surprise. She's usually too stressed from work and ordinarily doesn't have much free time. Shopping with her will be fun, and maybe she can help you choose the perfect pair of shoes.

A short time later, you try to decide which shoe store to check out first. There are seven in the mall, and each one looks promising.

Your mother goes into one called If the Shoe Fits.

As you start to follow her, you promptly collide with someone holding a stack of shoe boxes.

Shoes and boxes fly into the air. You cry out as your feet tangle and you fall backward.

The person you've collided with bends over you and asks, "Are you okay?"

"Huh?" you mumble, feeling like a complete klutz.

You brush your hair from your face and gaze into the most incredible chocolate brown eyes you've ever seen. And the face that goes with them is pretty incredible, too. The guy you're ogling is extremely cute.

And you just smashed into him!

*Turn to the **next page**.*

"I'm okay if you don't count being completely humiliated," you say, uncrossing your legs and feebly standing up.

As he puts his round tortoiseshell glasses back on, he steadies you with a firm, gentle hand. "I'm the one who should be sorry. I was trying to decide which pair of shoes to buy and wasn't watching where I was going."

You frown at the jumble of shoes and boxes around you. "What a mess. I'll help you straighten up."

"Thanks," he says, and you both get to work matching shoes with boxes.

"Are you buying all these shoes?" you ask.

"Nope. Just one pair." He points to a light tan pair. "Do you like these?"

"They're okay." You hand him a box with slick dark brown shoes. "These are better. They'll go great with your dark eyes."

"Really think so?"

You know your cheeks are reddening, but you nod anyway. "Yeah."

"Hey, thanks. I couldn't decide which pair to buy. Now you've made the decision for me. I like a girl who can make solid decisions." He grins. "By the way, my name is Devin. And your name is . . . ?"

*Turn to the **next page**.*

"There you are!" your mother interrupts. "I've found the most adorable shoes for you. They're available in gold, silver, and ruby red. You'll love them."

"But I was talking—" you sputter.

Your mother gives you a no-nonsense look. "Come look at these shoes now. The salesclerk is waiting for us."

You shrug apologetically to Devin, then go with your mother. You glance over your shoulder at Devin with a sense of loss. Your one chance with a cute, nice guy and you're stuck buying shoes. You don't know Devin's full name or where he goes to school. You'll never see him again, and he doesn't even know your name!

You spend the next thirty minutes slipping shoes on and off. You convince your mother that you need violet purple shoes, not gold, silver, or ruby red. You choose a pretty pair of purple pumps.

Your mother offers to treat you to an ice-cream brownie sundae, and you eagerly agree. You may have blown it with Devin, but spending the afternoon with your mother has been fun. And you can't wait to try out your new pumps on Emilee's dance floor.

X O X O X

Before you know it, it's party time! You're at Emilee's spectacular mansion with your dream date, Timothy. Well, he may not be your *dream* date, but at least you feel comfortable with him, and you know you'll both have fun.

*Turn to **page 88.***

♥ His lips taste sweet and you continue the kiss. Your mind has stopped working. Your conscience has packed its bags and left the country—maybe the universe!

You wrap your arms around Bill's shoulders and lean against him. He smells of musky cologne, and you feel like you could kiss him forever.

"Bill!" you hear someone scream, and instantly Bill pulls away from you.

You look toward the scream and immediately see Lori. You've never seen her look so outraged and angry in your life.

"What's going on?" Lori demands.

"Nothing!" Bill exclaims, shifting his gaze between you and Lori.

"I'm sorry," you say softly. You never meant to hurt her, and you feel rotten. You hope Lori can understand and forgive you.

But Bill has other ideas.

 *Turn to the **next page.***

"Lori," Bill says, coming over and taking her hand. "It wasn't my fault. She forced herself on me. I told her I wasn't interested, but she kissed me anyway."

"What!" you choke. "But that's not true!"

Lori aims a deadly stare at you. "I thought you were my friend."

"I am your friend. It's not what you—"

"How could you do this to me? I don't know what happened between you and Chad, but why hit on my guy?"

"I didn't . . . I mean . . . "

You sound dumb even to your own ears. The clouds in your brain clear, and you realize that Bill has made you look like an idiot.

Lori gives you one last dirty glance, then turns and leaves with Bill.

X O X O X

Two weeks later, Bill dumps Lori for Tara Lee Tracy.

Lori goes out with your old boyfriend, Nathan. She may be over Bill, but she hasn't forgiven you.

And you know she'll never completely trust you again.

The End

♥ You thank Alex for his invitation, then tell him no thanks. You just can't take the chance on a stranger over the phone. You'd rather play it solo—and safe.

So when Saturday night arrives, you're still dateless, but that's okay. You've decided to go with Lori and Bill.

"Two gorgeous girls just for me," Bill says, opening the back door of his car for you. Lori is already sitting in front, and Bill climbs in and drapes an arm around her shoulders. "Let's get movin'. It's party time!"

The words "party time" echo in your head. You cross your fingers and hope tonight turns out to be wonderful.

Bill drives through the massive gates and up a curvy tree-lined road. The car stops in front of the white, pillared, three-story mansion, and a parking attendant greets you.

"Welcome to the Chang estate," the attendant says, opening your car door. You feel like a movie star as you walk up the marble steps and enter Emilee's fabulous home.

A butler leads you through a tiled entryway and down a carpeted hallway. You admire framed portraits, crystal chandeliers, and unusual art pieces.

"This way, please," the butler says.

You hold your breath in eager anticipation.

At last, you're at the party!

*Turn to **page 30.***

♥ You just can't imagine spending a whole evening with Timothy. You decide to worry about a date later and head for the mall to shop for something to wear to the party.

As you step through the automatic glass door, you notice a group of guys hanging around an ornate marble fountain. You recognize one of the boys from your English class—tall, dark-haired Chad Estaban. He's balancing on the edge of the fountain, juggling soda cans. He's such a show-off—but a nice show-off. And ever since you helped him with a paper, you've been casual friends.

You remember your party invitation and look at Chad. He'd make a very fun date, but you've never gone out with him before, and you're nervous about asking him to the party. Your palms sweat and your heart beats rapidly.

You take a few steps forward, hesitating.

If you decide to ask Chad to Emilee's bash,
*turn to **page 31.***

If you decide to continue shopping,
*turn to **page 13.***

♥ Tears sting your eyes as you run from the room. The band is playing a song about broken hearts, and the sad words echo in your head as you race down a hallway. You're not sure where you're going . . . all you can think about is how much you hurt.

And you were really beginning to like Alex. Why did he have to go and spoil everything by two-timing you?

"Wait. Wait a minute!" someone shouts.

You pause on a staircase and glance back to see Alex running after you. How did he catch up with you so quickly?

You're too upset to face Alex, so you duck into a nearby doorway. Inside are an indoor star-shaped pool and steaming Jacuzzi.

Seconds later, Alex bursts through the doorway.

"So, here you are," Alex says.

"Just leave me alone."

He furrows his brow. "Why? Did I do something wrong?"

"Something wrong?" you shout, so irate you can't think straight.

"What?"

Fury builds within you until you can't take it anymore.

"I'll show you what!" You bring your hands together and shove Alex as hard as you can—right into the pool!

 Turn to the next page.

Alex yipes and splashes wildly in the water. "Hey! Why did you do that?"

"For the same reason you were dancing with Jennifer."

"Jennifer who?" he sputters, treading water.

"Don't lie! I saw you with Jennifer right after you told me you twisted your ankle and couldn't dance. But you're moving fine now!"

"I never hurt my ankle and I never danced with anyone but you. But I think I know what's been going on. I can explain!"

You're not interested in any more of his lies. You lower your eyes so Alex won't see your tears.

"I'm going home," you sniff.

"Please, don't," he says, breathing hard as he holds onto the pool rim. "Will you let me explain?"

"There's no excuse. I know what I saw."

"No. You don't."

You cross your arms over your chest and say stubbornly, "I suppose you're going to tell me it wasn't you. Like there's some other guy at this party who looks, talks, and is dressed exactly like you."

"That's right. My identical twin brother, Alan."

 *Turn to the **next page.***

You stare down at Alex, your jaw dropping in astonishment. "You have to be joking."

He shakes his wet head and grins. "Alan hid in the back of the van and crashed this party. I thought it was an easy way for him to see the famous Chang art collection. He's a major art fiend."

"You really do have a twin brother?"

Alex nods. "Sure do. Even our mother has trouble telling us apart. I told Alan to stay far from you, but he obviously messed up. I'm sorry."

"So *Alan* was dancing with Jennifer?" you ask, a slow smile spreading across your face.

"Yeah. And it was Alan who said those romantic things to you. I was worried that you might prefer him to me."

"I like *you*, Alex," you assure him.

"Whew! What a relief. I'm really sorry for not telling you about Alan."

"And I'm sorry for pushing you in the pool," you say. He looks so damp and soggy that you can't help but chuckle. But you feel really bad for dunking him. Suddenly you get an idea. . . .

Kicking off your shoes, you jump into the pool with him!

Alex laughs and swims over to you. You're laughing too, but not for long. Alex silences your laughter by holding you close and giving you a very sweet kiss.

The End

♥ The car roars through the intersection at the green light, sounding powerful and impressive. Timothy turns a corner, and the engine roars even louder. Perhaps too loud . . .

You notice smoke coming out from under the hood.

"The car's on fire!" you scream.

Timothy pulls over to the side of the road and slams on the brakes.

You jump out of the car and back away from the smoke. Your heart is now pounding in fear instead of happiness.

"Darn," Timothy mutters angrily. "I was afraid something was wrong with my car."

"Something's wrong, all right!" you cry. "Your car's burning up! It's going to explode!"

 *Turn to **page 62**.*

♥ Emilee has gone all out for this party. The five-member band is awesome. There are little colored lights strung everywhere. There's a scrumptious buffet, and an elaborate soda bar, too. The room is jamming with loud music and is filled wall-to-wall with party-goers.

"Cool," Timothy says. "I can't wait to hit the dance floor."

"Let's get something to drink first," you suggest tactfully. You remember Lori telling you some hilarious story about the last dance Timothy went to, where he made a complete fool of himself. He was only in seventh grade, but still . . .

Timothy walks to the soda bar, and you sit down at a table with Jennifer Wells. She's smart and pretty, and very quiet. She's also one of the best volleyball players—male or female—in the whole school.

While Timothy is busy ordering two sodas, you turn to Jennifer with a friendly smile. "Hi, Jennifer. Enjoying the party?"

She smiles back. "It's okay."

"Just okay?"

"Well . . . to be honest, I'm not having a very good time. I never should have come tonight."

"Why?" you ask.

 *Turn to the **next page**.*

She says sadly, "Because I don't have anyone to dance with."

"That's a bummer," you sympathize. You imagine how lonely going to a party solo could be.

"One cherry cola, as you ordered," Timothy says, coming over.

"Thanks." The drink is still fizzing, and it's cold and refreshing.

Timothy turns and notices Jennifer. A huge pleased smile spreads across his face. "Hi, there, Jen. Cut up any frozen worms lately?"

She blushes and giggles. "Not since last year. I'm surprised you remembered."

You glance between Jennifer and Timothy in confusion. Just how well do these two know each other?

Jennifer turns to you to explain. "Tim and I were biology partners last year."

Timothy adds, "Jennifer is the reason I aced the class."

"You would have done fine without me," she protests.

"But I wouldn't have had as much fun," he replies.

Timothy and Jennifer obviously like each other, and you feel like a third wheel with your own date. It crosses your mind that Timothy and Jennifer would rather be with each other. But where would that leave you?

 *Turn to the **next** page.*

Timothy is a terrific guy, and you've always considered him to be a good friend. You never really thought you'd date Timothy, but now that it's happened, you don't want to let him go. Even though you can see the sparks flying between Jennifer and him, Timothy is your date and you're not in a generous mood.

You set your empty glass down on the nearest table and say to Timothy, "I'm finished with my drink. Let's check out the rest of the party."

He nods. "Sure. It's been great talking, Jennifer."

You wave to Jennifer. "See you later."

"There's Emilee," you say, pointing to a dazzling dark-haired girl whirling on the dance floor with a tall, cute boy. "She and Tyler make a great couple, don't they?"

Timothy doesn't answer. He's not listening to you. Instead, he's staring at the retreating figure of Jennifer Wells.

 *Turn to **page 8**.*

♥ "I don't have a date, either," you admit.

Jennifer's eyes widen. "But I thought you were going out with Nathan."

"Not anymore." Your gaze drifts to the doorway, where you spot Nathan with Tara Lee. Your heart sinks down to your toes. You thought you were over Nathan, but seeing him with someone else hurts—a lot.

Jennifer pats your shoulder sympathetically. "I'm sorry. Want to talk about it?"

You watch Nathan take Tara Lee's hand and pull her to the dance floor. He spins her under his arm and snuggles her up against his chest.

A tear trickles down your cheek and you set your drink down. "Yeah. It's getting too crowded in here. Let's go somewhere else."

"I know just the place," she says. Then she explains that she's been to Emilee's house many times before. She lives nearby and practically grew up with Emilee.

Jennifer takes you to a large room with an indoor star-shaped pool and a Jacuzzi. You and Jennifer stretch out on plastic lounge chairs.

"Emilee and I used to spend hours in here when we were younger," Jennifer says. "But we don't see much of each other anymore. She's always busy."

"With Tyler?" you guess.

*Turn to the **next page**.*

"Yeah. I wouldn't mind if I had a boyfriend, too."

"Sounds like we both have the No-Beau Blues," you say.

Jennifer giggles. "A very serious ailment."

"Do you know a remedy, Dr. Wells?"

"How about a heavy dose of someone tall, dark, and devastating?"

"Don't I wish!" You breathe a heavy sigh.

"Why waste time wishing?" Jennifer says matter-of-factly. "Let's take some positive action."

"What?"

"Pick a cute guy and ask him to dance."

You shake your head. "Too risky. What if he says no?"

"Then ask someone else. I'm tired of missing out on all the fun. It's time to take charge of my own destiny. You, too."

"I can't do it."

"If I can find the courage, so can you. Would you rather sit and mope all night or ask a cute guy to dance?"

You think of Devin and Alex. Either guy could have been your dream date, but you blew it. Two strikes are already against you.

But asking a boy to dance is so scary. . . .

*If you decide to do nothing, turn to the **next page.***

If you decide to ask a boy to dance,
*turn to **page 42**.*

You stare into the serene water in the pool and shake your head. "Sorry, Jennifer. But I'd rather stay here for a while. Go find a terrific guy to dance with."

"Not without you."

"I'll be fine," you insist.

"Are you sure?" she asks.

"Definitely. You go ahead and have fun. I need to think for a while."

"About Nathan?" she probes.

You hate to admit you're moping over your old boyfriend, so you just shrug and say nothing.

After Jennifer leaves, you kick off your shoes and recline in a lounge chair. You stare at the crystal blue water, remembering your last and final date with Nathan.

You went to the county fair. You and Nathan ate corn dogs and cotton candy and shared a thick green pistachio shake. On the scary rides Nathan held you close and you felt safe.

Everything was going great—until the fireworks.

The night was lit with spectacular fiery lights, and the two of you sat on a grassy hill to watch the show. That was when Nathan suggested you both date other people.

The memory is too painful to think about, so you sit up to put your shoes on. You freeze when you hear loud voices.

*Turn to the **next page.***

You recognize Tara Lee's slender figure and long black hair. But the boy with her isn't Nathan—it's Bill Sweeney. You don't want them to see you, so you duck behind a marble counter.

"What an adorable pool," Tara Lee gushes in her soft Southern drawl. "I wish I'd brought my swimsuit."

"So do I," Bill says. "You'd look cute in a bikini."

Tara Lee giggles. "You big flirt. You're terrible."

"But irresistible," he replies smoothly.

From your hidden position, you watch Tara Lee drape her arm around Bill's waist. You can't believe your eyes! Tara Lee is two-timing Nathan, and Bill is two-timing Lori. The slimy, back-stabbing creeps!

"So where's your boyfriend?" Bill asks Tara Lee.

"Who cares? I thought Nathan was a babe, but he's more like a baby. He keeps talking about his old girlfriend. Really boring."

Bill caresses Tara Lee's long hair and says softly, "I promise not to be boring."

"I sure hope so," she replies, leaning against him.

Tara Lee tilts her head, and Bill leans down to kiss her. You're outraged.

Lori needs to know what a snake Bill is—but should you be the one to tell her?

*If you go to find Lori, turn to the **next page**.*

If you stay where you are,
*turn to **page 63**.*

You sneak out of the room and find Lori sitting in a cushioned chair on the outskirts of the dance floor. She looks bored and lonely.

She brightens when she sees you. "Finally a familiar face. Have you seen Bill?"

You bite your lip and glance away. Can Lori deal with the truth?

"I–I just saw him," you admit uneasily.

"Good!" she exclaims, standing. "I'm in a dancing mood and I need my guy. Where is he?"

"Uh, by the swimming pool. But he's . . . not alone."

Lori's face turns pale. "This should shock me, but it doesn't. I've always known Bill loved attention—lots of attention from lots of girls. But I believed him when he said he loved me."

"He's such a creep," you say, trying to console your friend.

"A wormy, sleazy, scummy lowlife," Lori adds furiously.

"You'll find someone else," you assure her. "Bill isn't worth the heartache."

"That's for sure!" she says, her eyes blazing. "Well, the jerk's blown it bigtime, and he's not getting off that easily. Take me to the pool."

You hesitate, then nod. "All right. Follow me."

 *Turn to **page 35.***

♥ "Timothy, I have a great idea," you say cheerfully.

"What?"

"You want to dance and I don't. Jennifer wants to dance, too. So why don't you and Jennifer dance together?"

"Really? You wouldn't mind?" he says, already looking around the room for that pale blond head.

As you both go to find Jennifer, you feel a warm sense of happiness. It's fun to play matchmaker.

Timothy goes up to Jennifer and taps her on the shoulder. "Would you like to dance?"

Her blue eyes sparkle. "I'd love to."

"Are you sure you're okay?" Timothy asks.

You shrug as if you don't have a care in the world. "Oh, don't worry about me. I'll find something to do."

But after Timothy and Jennifer leave, that warm feeling of happiness disappears. Everyone else is laughing, smiling, and having a great time. What are you going to do?

*Turn to the **next page**.*

You order another cherry cola from the soda bar and sit down in a plush velvet chair.

You smile wistfully as you watch Timothy spin Jennifer around in circles. Jennifer has the grace of a ballerina, and Timothy is wowing the crowd. He's so good he could be on MTV! Where did he learn to dance so well?

Other dancing couples catch your attention. Lori and Bill are having a great time, and so are Nathan and Tara Lee. Your gaze lingers on Nathan, and you feel a sharp pang of loss. You and Nathan used to have such fun together. But now he's snuggling close with snooty Tara Lee, and you're sitting on the sidelines. All alone.

The music changes tempo and starts to rock. Timothy slips into high gear, and you get dizzy watching him. Jennifer is a fantastic dancer and can match moves with Timothy.

You're happy for Timothy, but miserable for yourself.

Maybe you should leave the party.

You're about to go find a ride home when suddenly you hear someone calling your name.

 *Turn to the **next page**.*

It's Emilee, and you're happy she's spotted you.

"Hi, Emilee," you say shyly. You admire how her dark hair complements her black blazer and gold jewelry. She's totally gorgeous!

Emilee flashes a dazzling smile. "I just wanted to thank you."

"Thank me? For what?"

"For setting up Jennifer and Timothy. Not too many people know that Jen and I are like sisters. We grew up together and share tons of special memories."

"Really?" You set your drink down and stare at Emilee in surprise.

"What you did for Jennifer was very cool," Emilee says warmly. "She's so shy, she would never have asked Timothy to dance herself. And she's been crazy about him since last year."

"When they were biology partners?" you guess.

"That's right. Jen's been moping over him ever since, but she's never done anything about it. But now, thanks to you, she and Timothy are dancing together. And I'm so grateful. If there's anything I can do for you, just ask."

*Turn to the **next page**.*

"Know any cute available guys?" you half-tease.

"You bet!"

"I was just kidding," you say quickly. "There's been enough matchmaking for one night. Thanks, anyway."

"I won't take no for an answer. I've got the perfect guy for you."

"No blind dates," you say firmly.

But Emilee is equally as firm. "Come on, you'll love Tyler's cousin. D.J. is hanging out in the video arcade because he didn't have a date for tonight."

"Why didn't he have a date?" you ask, imagining the most unlikable boy in the universe. He probably has a wart poking from his nose, a pudgy belly, and curly poodle hair. With an IQ of 40 or 50, all he talks about is how wonderful he is and how he's a gift to women. Suddenly Emilee's voice brings you back from your blind date nightmare.

"D.J. doesn't date much," Emilee admits. "He spends a lot of his time working with environmental groups. He's a great artist, too!"

You sit with your hands clenched together around your empty soda glass and nervously await your fate.

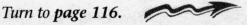

Turn to page 116.

 "I can't believe how much you and your brother look alike. No wonder I had such a hard time getting cherry colas," you say.

"Sorry about that. I left to talk to Alan, but then I couldn't find him."

"He was with me," you explain.

"Yeah," Alex says with a grimace. "Charming you with his romantic words."

"I thought he was you," you say with an amused smile.

"I don't know anything about poetic phrases. And I'm not into art like Alan."

"You like cars, right?" you ask, trying to sort out which brother said what.

Alex shrugs. "Yeah, but there's nothing romantic about cars. I know you were impressed when Alan compared your beauty to artwork. I'm sorry I'm not as good with words as my twin."

You feel flattered that Alex seems jealous of his own brother because of you. You take his hand and flash him a warm smile. "There's nothing to be sorry about."

*Turn to **page 52.***

♥ You set your cola down on a wicker table and take Nathan's hand in yours.

"Yes. I want to get back together with you. I guess I'm just crazy about you," you say, smiling.

Putting his drink aside, he wraps his arms around you. "And I'm even crazier about you."

"So we're both crazy," you tease, enjoying the warm, sturdy feel of Nathan. It's so nice to be next to him. You're glad you decided to take a chance on him.

"Think Timothy will mind?" he asks.

"He'll be happy for me. Anyway, it looked like he was having a great time with Jennifer. What about Tara Lee?"

"She's found someone new and doesn't care about me one bit. But she'll be furious, anyway."

You grin. Let Tara Lee stew about the one that got away—it'll serve her right!

You snuggle up against Nathan and sigh contentedly. "Emilee throws a great party, doesn't she?" you say.

"The greatest," he agrees.

Nathan stares into your eyes.

 *Turn to the **next page**.*

His lips lightly touch yours, and it feels like magic. You and Nathan are meant to be together, and you know you made the right decision.

Twenty years later, you and Nathan are a happy couple. He's a popular soap opera star, and you're his business manager. You travel around the world often with your two adorable children.

You and Nathan are deeply in love, and you both live happily ever after.

The End

♥ You dial the Cramers' number and Lori answers.

"Missed me already?" she teases.

"Actually, I wasn't calling you." You hesitate, feeling embarrassed. "I'd like to talk to Timothy."

"That's fantastic!" Lori cries happily.

"Don't get too excited," you caution. "Timothy could turn me down."

"Not a chance. I think he's secretly glad you broke up with Nathan. Hold on—I'll get him."

In the background you hear Lori calling her brother's name. You tap your fingers against your desktop and visualize Timothy. He's medium height and thin, with naturally wavy auburn hair. Faint freckles dot his nose, and his eyes are a clear hazel. His smile is sweet and he's very polite—always opening doors and pulling out chairs for people.

A second later, Timothy is on the line. Or at least you *think* he's on the line. You hear someone breathing, but nobody says anything.

"Timothy, are you there?" you ask.

"Yeah."

You smile in relief. It's Timothy, all right.

"Hi," you say. "I know this is sudden, but are you free Saturday night?"

*Turn to the **next page.***

"Free? Saturday?" Timothy asks.

"Yeah. Emilee Chang's having a fantastic party, and I'm supposed to bring a date. Do you want to go with me? Just as friends, of course."

"Yeah, that'd be fun," he says, and you notice a warmth in his tone you've never heard before.

You give Timothy the details, and he agrees to pick you up at six-thirty on Saturday.

You're excited about Emilee's party. Now that you have a date, your worries are over. Well, almost. You walk to your closet and flip through your clothes. You frown and wonder what you'll wear to Emilee's party. You need the *perfect* outfit.

You grab the casual purple tank dress you got last year and model it in front of the mirror. You look great, but you wonder if you should buy something new for the party.

*If you decide to shop for a dress, turn to **page 37**.*

If you decide to wear the purple dress,
*turn to **page 76**.*

♥ Sharing Chad's clown show with sick kids has been fun, but now that you think about it, you don't want to waste your Saturday night in a hospital. An opportunity to dance the night away at the Chang mansion is too wonderful to pass up.

So you take Chad's oversized gloved hand and lead him out of the hospital.

Soon you and your Bozo beau are walking into Emilee's palatial home. What an awesome place! You've never seen such an elaborate house. The chandeliers and ornate furniture take your breath away.

As you walk past the art gallery and a cozy den with a fireplace, you turn to Chad and say, "I'm sure Emilee can show you a good place to change. I'll go get us something to drink."

"I don't want to change." He stops abruptly. "Do you mind if I just leave on what I'm wearing?"

 *Turn to the **next page**.*

"A little bit," you admit. "Everyone is staring at us. Please change."

Chad says stubbornly, "I like how I look. Does it bother you that much?"

"It didn't bother me at the hospital. You were great with Ricky and the other kids. But nobody else is wearing a costume. Besides, with you in those huge duck feet, we won't even be able to dance!"

Anger flashes in Chad's dark eyes. "Well, take it or leave it," he threatens. "I'm not changing."

"You're being silly," you say. You can understand Chad's desire to be creative, but he's taking it too far. No one else at this party has duck feet and a red nose.

"Of course I'm silly. I'm a clown. Maybe you should find someone else to be your date."

"Maybe I will," you retort.

"Well good luck then!" Chad strides off, leaving you standing alone.

Now what are you going to do?

*Turn to the **next page**.*

You wander into the main room and order a cola from the soda bar. You spot Lori and Bill dancing under the colored lights. They seem to be having a good time—unlike you.

Several minutes later, Bill comes over and flashes you a wide grin. "Lori went to the ladies' room," he explains. "Want to dance with the best?"

"Who?" you tease.

He raises his chin proudly. "Me, of course."

"Sure. Why not?"

He leads you to the dance floor. Bill moves to the music and you go along with him. But you know you'll fade back to the sidelines as soon as Lori returns.

The band is great, and you begin to enjoy yourself. You notice Chad off in the distance blowing up balloons. He twists the long balloons into animal shapes and delights an adoring crowd of girls. Guess he's having fun in his own way . . . and you're having fun in yours.

The music slows and Bill pulls you close. He leans over and whispers, "You're looking great tonight. Where's your date?"

"Playing with balloons. It didn't really work out."

 *Turn to the **next page.***

"He must be crazy to desert you," Bill says, his warm breath sending tingles down your back.

"'Crazy' describes Chad exactly," you say, glancing around for Lori. Where is she, anyway?

"At least this gives us a chance to get to know each other better," Bill says, pulling you closer.

You pull back. Wait a minute—this is your best friend's boyfriend!

"We'd better find Lori," you say nervously.

"She can take care of herself."

"Maybe she can, but I don't know about myself."

"Just relax and dance," Bill says smoothly.

Your heart pounds and you feel warm. You realize you suddenly have this urge to kiss your best friend's boyfriend, so you turn and hurry away from the dance floor. You find a quiet outdoor patio and lean against a wicker chair.

Bill comes up behind you and says in a low, hurt voice, "Hey, why did you run off like that?" He gently touches your shoulders.

 *Turn to the **next page.***

You can't believe what's happening—and the worst part is that you're enjoying Bill's gentle touch. You've missed having a boyfriend, and Bill is being so sweet.

This is wrong! your conscience warns.

You whirl away from Bill. "Back off, Bill. You already have a girlfriend, remember?"

"I'd rather forget that for the moment. You're special, and I've wanted to kiss you for a long time." His gaze melts into yours and he pulls you toward him. Bill cups your chin in his hand and brings his lips down on yours. . . .

*If you enjoy the kiss, turn to **page 80.***

*If you slap Bill's face, turn to **page 12.***

♥ "We'll talk after we enter the contest," you say, pulling him to the end of the line.

"All right. But afterwards, we talk."

"I promise," you say.

When you reach the beginning of the line, Emilee hands you a skinny piece of red rope candy.

"Licorice?" Nathan says. "What's this for?"

Emilee smiles mysteriously. "You'll find out."

You glance curiously at the spiral candy. "Only one for the two of us?" you ask Emilee.

Her smile widens and her eyes sparkle. "That's what makes this game fun."

You and Nathan wait until Emilee has finished handing out licorice ropes to each couple.

*Turn to the **next page.***

You look at Nathan and warm feelings fill you. This is just like old times: you and Nathan together.

"Attention everyone," Emilee calls, standing on the stage in front of the band. "Ready for something sweet?"

Shouts of "yes!" roar through the room.

"Then organize in lines, facing your partner. I've placed judges around the room—one judge for every ten couples. Each group will have one winning couple."

"What's the licorice for?" someone shouts.

"For eating!" Emilee answers. "Each of you puts an end of the piece of licorice in your mouth. The first couple to finish their licorice wins the contest."

You face Nathan, your heart pounding. You slowly put one end of the sweet cherry licorice in your mouth and wait. . . .

*Turn to the **next page**.*

Emilee shouts, "Go!" and the candy race is on.

You're chewing and swallowing as fast as you can. The licorice slips out of Nathan's mouth once, but he quickly resumes munching.

Suddenly there's no more candy . . . but there is Nathan. His lips press softly against yours, and dimly you hear someone shouting, "You've won!"

Your head spins and you feel like you can't breathe. All you can think about is Nathan and how great it is to be with him.

"Congratulations!" Lori cries, pulling you away from Nathan. "Aren't you thrilled?"

Lori's holding a half-eaten piece of licorice in her hand. "Bill and I got sick of the candy, but we enjoyed the kissing part. Looks like you and Nathan enjoyed that part, too."

You smile shyly at Nathan. Being with him is great. Even if you had lost the contest, you still would have been a winner.

"Timothy and Jennifer each won a CD for the dance contest," Lori chatters on. "I wonder what kind of prize Emilee will give you guys."

*Turn to the **next page**.*

Three other couples are winners, too. You all go to the stage for your prizes.

Emilee pulls out a box with four small, festively decorated baskets. She waves one basket and shows off the wrapped goodies. "Each winning couple receives a Chang specialty basket. For candy lovers, I've included two packages of licorice."

The crowd snickers.

Emilee reaches in and pulls out two scraps of paper. "Also, each winner will enjoy a set of tickets."

"To a rock concert?" one girl onstage asks hopefully.

"Guess again," Emilee says with a laugh. "These tickets are for a new play about Casanova called *The Kissing Bandit*."

The crowd hoots and hollers. You squeeze Nathan's hand and think how great going to a romantic play with him will be. Of course, there might be more kissing in the audience than onstage.

"And finally," Emilee says, waving a small package in the air, "something for the end of a romantic date."

Noisy whispers echo and all eyes are on Emilee. You try to see what she's holding, but it's wrapped in shiny paper with a tiny metallic ribbon.

You wonder what this final item will be. . . .

*Turn to the **next page**.*

Emilee rips off the wrapping paper dramatically. "Chapstick!"

The entire room bursts into boisterous laughter. You accept your prize basket and step down from the stage. Your hand lingers in Nathan's, and you follow him to a quiet patio.

"So are we finally going to talk?" he asks, staring deeply into your eyes.

You want Nathan to love you again more than anything, but you're afraid to admit it.

He continues to look at you, but there's something new in his gaze. Your heart speeds up as you realize he's afraid of being hurt, too. Maybe breaking up was as hard on him as it was on you.

"What do you want to discuss?" you ask, meeting his gaze.

"You and me. Us," he replies. "Is there still an *us?*"

 *Turn to the **next page**.*

You nod, then reach into your prize basket. Flashing a warm smile, you wave a red spiral of licorice in front of his face. "We can talk more later. Right now I feel like something sweet. Want to share a piece of licorice?"

Nathan answers by placing one end of the licorice in his mouth.

Within seconds, the candy disappears . . . and in its place is a new start for romance.

For the second time in one night, you're a winner.

The End

♥ Emilee returns a few minutes later . . . alone.

You breathe a heavy sigh of relief. Guess she couldn't pry D.J. from his video game.

"So where's D.J.?" you ask.

"He'll be here soon. He said something about wanting to reach level nine on his game, but he's very excited about meeting you."

"Oh," you say with no excitement in your tone.

"D.J.'s a great guy. I just know you two will hit it off."

"Uh huh," you murmur, unconvinced.

Emilee tosses her black hair over one shoulder and suddenly points. "Oh, here comes D.J. now!"

You brace yourself and slowly turn to look at D.J.

"YOU!" you choke, unable to believe your eyes.

 *Turn to the **next page.***

It's Devin from the shoe store!

"Hi," D.J. (alias Devin) says with a huge grin. "Nice pair of shoes."

"I like yours, too. Brown was a good choice," you say, barely noticing that Emilee has walked away.

Devin stares into your eyes. Your heart pounds faster than the music the band is playing. You're so glad to see Devin again.

"Finding you here is a nice surprise," he says. "I usually don't agree to blind dates, but it was hard to say no to Emilee."

You giggle. "I know what you mean. I don't usually agree to blind dates, either. But this time I'm glad I did."

"Me, too." He steps closer and gently takes your hand.

"I guess the D in D.J. stands for Devin," you say.

 *Turn to the **next page**.*

"That's right. And I'll tell you what the J stands for . . . if you'll dance with me," he says flirtatiously.

"Is that an invitation?" you tease.

"You bet." He grins. "What's your answer?"

You meet his grin with a sweet, sassy smile. "The answer's yes."

Then, hand-in-hand, you go off to the dance floor with your new dream date.

The End

♥ You watch the dancers and see several familiar faces, including your old boyfriend, Nathan. He's with Tara Lee Tracy. They look stunning together, but for the first time since you and Nathan broke up, your heart isn't ripping apart when you see him.

You're happy with your own date. Although you met via a wrong number, in your opinion there's not a thing wrong with Alex.

"Did you miss me?" Alex asks, handing you a glass of cherry cola and sitting down beside you.

"Terribly," you say with a smile. "Thanks for the drink."

"No problem. I would have been back sooner, but I ran into an old friend."

"Girl or guy?" you ask.

His hazel eyes twinkle. "A guy. But if I had said a girl, would you be jealous?"

"Only if you told her that her beauty belongs on a canvas, too."

"A canvas? Like a portrait?" He chuckles. "Too artsy for my taste."

You give Alex a puzzled glance. "But you're the one who compared my looks to art."

*Turn to the **next page**.*

"And I meant every word," he replies quickly.

"I'm glad. Most guys would be embarrassed to say romantic things. But then you're not 'most guys'—which is what makes you so special."

"You think romantic guys are special?" He frowns and swallows the remainder of his cola. Setting his empty glass down, he stands up. "I'm still thirsty. Think I'll go get a refill. Do you want another cherry cola?"

"No. But I'm itching to dance again, so hurry back."

He smiles. "I promise."

You watch him turn the corner and disappear from sight.

Barely two minutes later, he's back with a drink and gives you another cherry cola.

You stare at him, trying to decide if he's kidding or just terribly forgetful.

"Is something wrong?" Alex asks, his tone courteous and concerned.

"This is a joke, right?" You point to the cherry cola you're still drinking. "Didn't you just leave to get yourself a refill?"

"I did? Yeah. That's right, I did." He slaps his forehead and grins sheepishly. "Guess I got confused."

"That's okay. Forget the drinks. Let's dance."

*Turn to the **next page**.*

You go out to the dance floor, squeezing in next to Lori and Bill. Lori gives you the "thumbs up" sign, letting you know she approves of Alex.

The band switches to a rap number, and Alex moves awkwardly. He's not as smooth as he was earlier. He steps on his own foot, stumbles, and falls against you.

"Ouch! I twisted my ankle!" he cries, hobbling away from the dance floor and sinking into a chair.

"Are you all right?"

"I think so. Rap music isn't my thing."

You sit next to him. He moans, and you ask, "Are you in pain?"

"A little. I'd better go in the bathroom and check for swelling. I won't be long."

"That's okay. I don't mind waiting," you say, trying to hide your disappointment.

You get up from the chair and glance around the dance floor.

 *Turn to the **next page**.*

Your gaze sweeps over the dance floor and you recognize Jennifer Wells—she's in one of your classes. You've always thought she was intelligent and nice, but now as you watch her sway gently to a slow beat, you also admire her elegant beauty.

Jennifer's pale head rests against her partner's shoulder. You can't see her partner's face, but something about his build and his curly brown hair is familiar.

Jennifer spins away, then back into her partner's arms. You stare in stunned astonishment.

Jennifer is dancing with Alex!

If you confront Alex, turn to the **next page.**

If you leave the room, turn to **page 84.**

You stomp over to Alex and grab his arm. "What do you think you're doing?" you demand furiously.

Alex blinks, as if he's confused. "I'm dancing. Have you met Jennifer?"

"I know who she is!" you snap. "But I don't know why you bothered to lie about hurting your leg. If you didn't want to dance with me, you should have been honest."

Jennifer drops Alex's hand and gives him an angry look. "Is this true? But you told me you didn't have a date."

Alex glances helplessly between the two of you. "I didn't . . . I mean . . . it's complicated."

"There's nothing complicated about ditching your date to dance with another girl!" you yell.

Alex backs away from the dance floor, but you and Jennifer follow him. "I want an explanation," you insist.

"I didn't mean to hurt anyone," Alex says, looking highly uncomfortable.

"You lied to both of us," Jennifer says.

"You're a disgusting, dishonest, totally slimy two-faced creep, Alex Reed-Cohen!" you accuse.

He rubs his forehead and says wearily, "You've got it all wrong. My name isn't Alex . . . it's Alan."

 *Turn to **page 41**.*

♥ "You okay?" Timothy whispers as a butler opens the door and leads you down a long portrait-lined hallway.

"Of course."

"You don't sound okay. And you look miserable."

"I'm fine," you snap, immediately wishing your voice hadn't been so harsh. Timothy has been nothing but a good friend, and it's not his fault you can't keep Nathan out of your mind.

Music blares from a live band on a raised stage. There's a huge buffet and a soda bar, too. The center of the room sparkles with colored lights strung over a crowded dance floor. The room quakes from the noise, and you have to scream to be heard.

"Do you want something to eat?" you yell to Timothy.

"Not yet. Let's dance."

"No," you say quickly. Lori warned you about the last dance Timothy went to—his seventh grade spring dance, where he stepped on a girl's foot and tripped her, then stepped on her dress and ripped a huge hole in the back! Sure, it's been five years since the embarrassing event, but why take chances?

"Why not?" Timothy asks.

"Well . . ." You pause to think of a good excuse.

*Turn to the **next** page.*

You look around and catch a glimpse of Emilee Chang. "I want to thank Emilee for inviting us. Come with me."

You and Timothy weave through the crowd, murmuring "excuse me's." When you get close enough to call out to Emilee, you stop and stare. You've seen that sophisticated outfit before—in fact, you almost bought it from Bodacious Boutique.

Anger spreads through you as you think back to how "helpful" Tara Lee was in the store. That sneaky Tara Lee purposely tried to sell you the same blazer and leggings Emilee Chang had undoubtedly already purchased. And you almost fell for it! It's a good thing you trusted your own common sense and ignored Tara Lee's advice.

"Is something wrong?" Timothy asks with concern.

"Something almost was, but everything's fine now."

"Are you going to talk to Emilee?"

"Maybe later. She's busy dancing with her boyfriend, Tyler."

Timothy pulls you close and says, "Dancing sounds like a great idea."

You hesitate and try to decide what to do. How can you get out of dancing?

If you say you want to find Lori,
*turn to the **next page**.*

If you say you want something to drink,
*turn to **page 21**.*

"I need to talk to Lori for a minute," you blurt out.

Timothy isn't wild about hanging out with his sister, but he goes along while you search for Lori. You spot her standing alone, watching everyone dance.

"Hi, Sis," Timothy says. "Where's your other half?"

"Around somewhere." She shrugs and smiles. "I can't keep track of Bill. He has so many friends, I keep losing him. But when I find him, we're going to hit the dance floor. The band is so cool."

"I agree," Timothy says. "I've been trying to convince my date to dance, but she keeps making excuses."

"No, I don't!" you protest, embarrassed that Timothy can read you so well.

Timothy grins. "Then prove it. Let's dance."

You smile and nod. "Okay, okay. Lead me to the dance floor."

Turn to page 67.

Look for . . .

Pick Your Own Dream Date
spring **break!**

Get ready for an awesome week filled with fun in the sun in *Spring Break!*, the second title in the hot new series *Pick Your Own Dream Date*. With friends Emilee and Jennifer, you'll head to Misty Shores, California, where you can go horseback riding on the beach, bodysurf in the ocean, snuggle around a midnight bonfire, and enjoy other romantic adventures.

You'll meet new possible dream dates, such as shy Andrew Bellente, an aspiring artist, as well as his cousin Jason Hart, the gorgeous lifeguard of Misty Shores. You'll also meet up with flirtatious Bill Sweeney, and if you're lucky, you may run in to dream date Devin Vargas. And what about your on-again, off-again boyfriend Nathan Fields?

Pick Your Own Dream Date

Choose your favorite guy!
Pick from 17 possible endings.

spring **break!**

By
Linda Joy Singleton

Get set for adventure (definitely!) and romance (who knows?) as you head out on your *Spring Break!*

ABOUT THE AUTHOR

Linda Joy Singleton has written several books for both young adults and middle grade readers. She lives near Sacramento, California, with her husband and two children. She enjoys walking, boating, camping, reading, square dancing, and collecting books for girls, such as the *Nancy Drew* and *Judy Bolton* series. She also loves animals and has lots of pets, including ducks, geese, cats, dogs, goats, and an Appaloosa horse named Stormy.